The Totem

The Totem

Marguerite Primeau
Translated by
Margaret M. Wilson

Ekstasis Editions

Canadian Cataloguing in Publication Data

Primeau, Marguerite
    The Totem.

    ISBN 1-896860-79-6

    I. Title.
    Ps8576.O724C66   2002   C811'.54   C00-911226-X
    PR9199.3.M649C66   2002

© Marguerite Primeau, 2001.
Cover Art: Noreen Taylor

© Marguerite Primeau and Edition des Plaines, 1986, 2001
Translation © Margaret Mary Wilson, 2001

The original French, *Le Totem* was published in St Boniface,
Winnipeg by Editions des Plaine.

Published in 2002 by:
Ekstasis Editions Canada Ltd.
Box 8474, Main Postal Outlet   Box 571
Victoria, B.C. v8w 3s1   Banff, Alberta tol oco

THE CANADA COUNCIL | LE CONSEIL DES ARTS
FOR THE ARTS | DU CANADA
SINCE 1957 | DEPUIS 1957

BRITISH
COLUMBIA
ARTS COUNCIL
Supported by the Province of British Columbia

The translation of *The Totem* has been done with the assistance of the Canada
Council for the Arts Translation Program. *The Totem* has been published
with the assistance of a grant from the Canada Council for the Arts and the
Cultural Services Branch of British Columbia.

Contents

The Totem

She drew her chair closer to the fire. It was watching her from the mantelpiece. She could feel it right through to her bones.

She focused on the meagre flames struggling to tease some thin green branches into life. She had cut them herself from the apple tree, against the doctor's orders. But, as if pulled by an invisible thread, her lowered glance was drawn upwards till it rested on the native totem carving, still in its place on the chimney piece.

It was watching her.

She shivered, as much from the cold that had invaded the room as from the mysterious gaze that bore down on her.

Pulling the old blue cardigan tighter around her, she noticed once again that it was fraying all over, its worn fabric a maze of darns. Still, it gave her the illusion of warmth even if this evening it took a strong effort of will. She began examining her cardigan again, to take her mind off the figurine which seemed to emanate contempt from its place on the mantelpiece, and its disturbing sculpted black stone creatures: Eagle and Raven at the top and crouching at the very bottom, Frog.

This old blue sweater, when and where had she bought it? She had forgotten that she had never bought it. It had belonged to her half sister, that scatterbrain, Mariette. After Mariette's sudden death she had decided that it was still good enough for her to use even though it was too tight across her shoulders.

"It'll be warmer," she had decided.

It never crossed her mind to give it to the Salvation Army for the poor or to the St. Vincent de Paul Society.

The poor? They'll always be with us. Christ himself said so. In any case, wasn't she poor too? Income taxes were eating away at her retired secretary's pension. And as for the few dividends she received every month, the State devoured at least a quarter of them. And the taxes on her house and little bit of garden! And… there had been Mariette!

The poor. She was part of their brotherhood, except they didn't pay income taxes.

So, she had kept the cardigan. She cut off the frayed edges, she darned the holes, she replaced the lost buttons with others that more or less matched. To tell the truth, she had never seriously considered replacing it.

"Woollens are outrageously expensive," she told herself every time the thought came up. It can last a few more months. I'll wait for the next sales.

And the matter was settled once more.

To be frank, she didn't have an ounce of vanity. Not

an ounce. Had she ever had any? One day? A long time ago? She certainly wouldn't have been able to say. All that was so far in the past, so dead.

She lifted up the twisted bits of branch with the tongs, built them into a kind of pyramid and blew on the embers.

She was soon out of breath.

She shouldn't have tackled the apple tree. The neighbour's gardener wouldn't have turned down a few dollars to prune it.

But that's what had deterred her, what always deterred her. Spending money for a mere nothing, for no reason. That was her taboo. It wasn't as far removed as she would have liked to believe from the so-called sacred status that Mariette attributed to the totem. It was just as inviolable, the object of unfailing respect and the same meticulous attention that Mariette had lavished on her black sculpture.

She was no longer young but she could still climb the ladder and use the secateurs.

But this morning the pain had come back again, stabbing behind her ribs, forcing her to stop and catch her breath.

Once her breathing became easier she went back to work, putting what she considered a moment of weakness out of her mind.

If she had to give in and hire someone every time she felt the slightest bit ill, what would be left of her savings? Inflation was eating away at the dollar, the cost of living was going up from one month to the next. Soon she would have nothing left…except the totem!

She cast a quick glance at it, automatically calculating what she could get for it now – four thousand dollars the gallery manager had said. But confronted with what, in the half darkness, seemed to her a series of glowering masks, she quickly looked away.

She had never pampered herself. She wasn't going to start now. Once it was gone money wouldn't reappear in the spring like the leaves on the apple tree. In spite of what Mariette may have thought.

And then there was the medicine. Digitalis wasn't cheap. For finally she had had to see the doctor. He told her she had heart problems. She would have to be careful from now on, avoid all strenuous work. He gave her a prescription and told her to stick scrupulously to the prescribed dosage. That didn't stop her from cheating, pretending to forget to take her pills, skipping a day and sometimes two on the pretext that she felt better. A little bit more money to put aside for a rainy day.

She let her head rest on the back of the armchair, making herself breathe gently, slowly.

"That's worth all the doctors' remedies," she told herself. "And it doesn't cost as much."

But the pain persisted. If she had had a telephone she would have called someone, her neighbour, anyone at all so as not to stay alone with her pain…and the totem. But she hadn't had a telephone since the day the company increased the price of its services. And this evening the totem shone with a secret, malevolent life.

From the stony gaze of Eagle, Raven, Wolf and the

woman held in Bear's clasp down to Frog's bulging eyes, an occult power was taking over, holding her captive to its mystery.

Besides, who could she call on? The neighbours went about their business, just as she did. Their relationship was limited to a quick hello when she happened to meet one of them.

Not like Mariette, who, as soon as she arrived had set about making friends among the people who lived on Twelfth Avenue overlooking the calm waters of Burrard Inlet.

Jeanne tried to curb what she saw as foolishness, given Mariette's circumstances. She wanted to make her understand that friends are always costly. They either encourage you to be extravagant, take a trip to California – which Mariette had done in spite of Jeanne's remonstrances (as she watched her half-sister's modest income melt away like snow in the sun) – or go to the theatre, the movies, or on outings to Vancouver Island or the Sechelt Peninsula. And goodness knows what else! And then there were the vagaries of fashion. For how can one arrive for cocktails at the lovely, Greek-style villa at the far end of the street, wearing a three year-old skirt? And how can one go cross-country skiing without an outfit just as elegant as the ones our friends wear? And jogging? What a joke! The very latest jogging suit cost at least a hundred and fifty dollars, and eighty dollar sport shoes! All that money wasted to get out of breath running from one street to another. It almost made Jeanne ill.

Mariette went through her salary in the first few days

and counted on her numerous credit cards to make it to the end of the month. Jeanne knew all about that because, after Mariette's death, she had had to repay the stores, at the highest interest rates of course.

The only thing Mariette and her husband had lived for was to have fun. And Devil take the consequences! Paul, who was an agent in a sports car sales company, spent his days driving prospective clients around in the latest model convertible. Mariette often accompanied him although it was against the rules. Or else, right in the middle of a working day, they would set out for the suburbs or the mountains, hair blown by the wind, their faces sunburnt or rosy from the fresh air. Jeanne hardly saw them. Since her big-sisterly advice was never welcome, Mariette didn't regret the infrequency of her visits, and Paul even less so.

Paul died in a car accident. A lovely blue convertible that Mariette adored. Paul, who always drove at the speed limit when he didn't go over it, missed a turn in the mountains one rainy night. They were found at the bottom of a ravine under a tangle of blue metal. Paul, his chest crushed, had been killed outright – Mariette got away with bruises and a broken arm. A month later, with her arm healed, she started to enjoy life again and came to live on Twelfth Avenue.

Mortgaged down to the last brick, their villa in the mountains with a view of the Gulf Islands was sold by the creditors, and the mahogany furniture, the blue silk covered chair – Mariette loved that colour, it brought out her blond hair – all disappeared under the auctioneer's hammer.

She arrived at Jeanne's with a suitcase and a First Nation's totem wrapped up in the blue cardigan. Carved from the black stone of the Queen Charlotte Islands, the figurine had been a gift from her father, who bought it from a Haida. Her father had made Mariette promise never to be separated from it, as the sculptor had invested it with the Haida tribe's protective powers.

Mariette firmly believed that she had been saved thanks to the intervention of Raven and Eagle, whereas Paul, who had always laughed at what he called a savage's superstition, had died. So she had managed to hide the totem from the auctioneer the day he came to list the contents of the villa. It had stood on the mantelpiece ever since, the focal point of the room, mocking Jeanne who had immediately sensed the sales value of the argillite figurine.

One day when Mariette, a salesclerk in a supermarket, was out, Jeanne had the sculpture appraised. The native art expert offered her two thousand dollars. Apparently, the totem was authentic, the work of an old Haida carver, famous in his time.

Jeanne was dumbfounded. She promised herself to convince Mariette to part with the totem. Two thousand dollars wasn't to be sniffed at. And, if the expert's apparent delight and the gentleness with which he stroked the sculpture were anything to go by, Jeanne would probably be able to get more for it.

Her suspicions aroused, Mariette attacked Jeanne as soon as she brought up the subject.

"What do you think you're meddling in? That totem is mine," she shouted, "and don't you dare lay a finger on it. Besides," she added, with a nasty look, "who told you? And how do you know what it's worth?"

Jeanne had, however, been extremely careful. She hadn't said anything that might imply she knew anything about the subject. On the contrary, she had mentioned in passing:

"I saw in the newspaper the other day that there was a sale of native art in town. They even had some photos. And, you know, none of the totems in the ad was as beautiful as yours."

And, since Mariette was looking at her without a word:

"Maybe it would be a good idea to know how much it's worth… You never know…"

"The paper?" Mariette interrupted, "Since when do you get the paper? I've never seen a single one in this house. Where do you hide them?"

Try as she might to explain that she had stopped in front of the grocer's that sold the morning paper and that she had seen the advertisement there, she didn't fool Mariette who burst out laughing, then got angry.

"Don't you dare meddle with my totem," she repeated. "It saved my life. It's my protector, you hear, the protector of the poor widow that I am now."

And she burst into tears.

Her tears failed to move Jeanne, who muttered to herself that Raven and Eagle might well have protected her half-sister from a husband who let the money flow through his fingers like water in a stream. They could have stopped them from getting up to their necks in debt so Jeanne wouldn't have had to house Mariette for next to nothing. The rent Mariette paid her was barely enough since she, Jeanne, was landed with all the maintenance costs, heat, electricity, the phone etc. It didn't even occur to Mariette to contribute to the ever-increasing expenses.

She, in turn, lost her temper.

"All you think about is having fun," she shouted. "You don't have the least idea, you don't even want to know what it means to have slaved all your life, economized, counted every penny day in day out, year after year to make ends meet… to stay out of debt… to owe nothing to anybody."

She paused for a moment.

"So as not to end up being a burden to anyone."

Mariette was having none of it.

"Don't come crying to me," she said, coldly. "You've worked, I realize that. But what you don't say is that you're obsessed with penny pinching. It's your whole life now. You get as much pleasure out of it as a drunk gets from his bottle."

She went on in a conciliatory tone:

"You've invested your money well. If you wanted to you could live very comfortably, enjoy life a bit. We could even take a trip together. How does Christmas in Hawaii sound to you?"

But, faced with Jeanne's stubborn expression, she shrugged her shoulders impatiently.

"Don't look at me as if I'm talking nonsense. I wasn't born yesterday, you know. And don't forget that you inherited the house from our mother and, contrary to what you would have me believe, it didn't cost you a cent."

She twisted a bit of perfumed handkerchief in her hands.

"And you want to take what little I have away from me. My totem! You'll sell it over my dead body. I don't judge everything in terms of dollars. You have a right to do as you wish. Just don't expect me to do the same. I prefer to live instead of counting pennies."

She ran and shut herself in her room. Shortly afterwards, she emerged with a smile.

Jeanne was left to nurse her anger alone. She would have liked to remind her half-sister that the house had been left to both of them and that Mariette had preferred to sell Jeanne her share because she and Paul needed the money.

Jeanne never knew what the considerable sum she had given her was used for. It had probably been swallowed up in some business venture that had gone sour. For Paul, who always believed he was just about to become a millionaire, didn't hesitate to invest in the most dubious affairs as long as they were tempting.

So the totem stayed in its place on the mantelpiece. It was still there, even though Mariette had been felled by a ruptured aneurysm three years earlier while skiing.

Maybe because she was afraid of bringing bad luck on herself – for it was no use telling herself that Eagle and Raven had been supremely indifferent to Mariette's fate

– or maybe because she had guessed that argillite fig-
urines were becoming increasingly rare, and consequent-
ly more and more sought after, Jeanne was waiting for
the right moment to sell it. At the local library she leafed
through the periodicals that devoted a few pages to
native art in the hope of finding out the approximate
value of the totem. Surely it would fetch more than two
thousand dollars now. Finally, she had gone to an exhi-
bition of First Nations' sculptures. From Jeanne's
description, the name of the Haida sculptor and the date
of the figurine, the curator suggested something around
four thousand dollars, but nevertheless reserved the right
to change his mind after examining the statuette.

After months of deliberation, torn between the fear
of offending she wasn't quite sure whom and the thought
of an investment of four thousand dollars at eighteen per
cent, she had called him that afternoon from the nearest
phone booth. They had made an appointment for the
next day.

Jeanne had to admit it was a truly beautiful sculpture even though, at that moment, she hardly dared even
glance at the constantly shifting reflections, reminiscent
of the aurora borealis, flitting across the figurine's black
surface.

A light flickered in the depths of the stone eyes. And
suddenly Jeanne remembered the will o' the wisps that
were said to emanate from the mire of the swamps.

Yet Mariette, who was fascinated by tribal mytholo-
gy, had maintained that Eagle and Raven had protective
powers, and Bear, against which a female silhouette nes-

17

tled, wasn't in the least bit threatening. She had quite simply said, "the Bear Mother" and offered no other explanation. Jeanne, for whom Haida sculpture was no more than one more source of money to be exploited, had made no effort to learn more about it.

Try as she might to repeat to herself that a totem was no use to anyone unless it was converted into hard cash, that it was ridiculous to want to attribute supernatural powers to animals, she felt no less a prisoner of the black figurine that was imperceptibly transforming itself before her eyes.

To break the spell which had made her almost forget that the pain had now spread as far as her shoulders, she set herself to examining the statuette in minute detail.

But the Eagle with its folded wings, which she had seen every day for years and had sometimes admired but more often disdained, as she did everything that wasn't a source of income, was no longer the "everyday" one. It's wings outstretched to their full span, it was gradually bearing down on her. To protect her? Oh no! More likely to attack her. Mariette had maintained that Lãg.a/Am, Raven's companion on his journeys, was a powerful supernatural being. Like Raven, he was part of the tribe's ancestry and, like Raven too, he was the one who decided each person's destiny. We owed him respect and devotion, something Jeanne had never given him.

Nanki IsLas, the Raven, was even more powerful. He was the Voice that commands, who stole the sun which he then gave to man. In the semi-darkness there was a cruelty about him that she had never seen before. His broad beak, narrowing to a sort of hook, seemed only to be waiting to tear apart human flesh.

The Voice that commands? Nanki IsLas? What was the Voice ordering him to do? Had Eagle and Raven already decided her destiny?

The wolf, with its meek air, its small, fan-shaped ears, its guileless eyes that had always amused her, invariably reminding her of the kind animal Little Red Riding Hood met in the forest, was reverting to its true characteristics or so it certainly seemed to Jeanne, hypnotized by its fiery red gaze.

Now the female figure was twisting in Bear's embrace. And, at the very bottom, Frog was laughing.

"What's going on? What's going on?" Jeanne repeated, transfixed, not daring to move for fear of setting in motion these animals that had a grudge against her without her knowing why.

"Mariette, Mariette," she cried suddenly.

Her voice echoed for a moment round the room.

In the fireplace, all that remained of the fire were a few bits of dead branches covered by a grey shroud of cinders. It was completely dark. Jeanne had forgotten to light the lamp.

Seized by panic, she got up suddenly. She had to do something, anything at all, to flee these eyes from beyond the grave! But she lost her balance and had to lean against the mantelpiece.

Her fingers, their joints deformed by age and arthritis, slid unconsciously towards the black stone totem. She seized it greedily, as if by doing so, she would succeed in exorcising the demons that inhabited it.

"Tomorrow," she gasped, "no later than tomorrow, I'm going to get rid of you. You can go and frighten someone else. Lãg.a⧸ Am... Nanki IsLas... and you too Wolf, you traitor, and you, Frog, with your grin."

Her lips twisted into a grimace.

"You're going to make me four thousand dollars. Do you hear? Four thousand dollars! That'll pay for the fright you've just given me."

All of a sudden, she fell, clutching the figurine.

"Four... thousand... dollars... Do you hea...."

Suddenly, a branch cracked at the back of the hearth. Then all was silent again.

Grandmother's Thousand "Hail Marys"

S taring into my glass of Vouvray many years after her death, I remembered my grandmother's thousand "Hail Marys."

It was Christmas Eve. I had just visited Chenonceau with some Canadian friends who had recently arrived in France. After trying to decipher the old castle's motto, *S'il vient à point, me souviendra,* and lingering over the splendour of its rooms, we had gone back to Tours more or less in silence.

Was it the contrast between this castle, "the castle of six women," and our province's hastily erected buildings that troubled us? Or was the mysterious motto playing on the feelings of three Canadians who suddenly felt homesick?

S'il vient à point, me souviendra.

Wanting to recapture the high spirits we had lost somewhere along the way, we treated ourselves to the best of Christmas Eve celebrations when we got back.

That's how, while I was savouring the Vouvray and the mussels, my grandmother suddenly appeared, her rosary in her hand, with Grandfather and all of us children reciting with her the thousand Christmas Eve "Hail Marys," more or less willingly.

My grandmother was the kind of old-style Quebecker that we don't find any more.

Her priest's word, whether on the subject of the weather or religion, was, for her, the Holy Gospel. It was mass every morning and the Blessed Sacrament in the afternoons. Right up till the day that death took her unawares.

How had such a distant memory risen to the surface of my glass of Vouvray?

Because my grandmother was pure Vouvray. Sweet, sparkling, even bubbly under her crown of white hair, she had exactly that hint of piquant we find in a Vouvray that pleasantly teases the palate before making your senses spin. This touch of mischief, which seemed innocent at first, invariably helped her to triumph over Grandfather, my mother and we children. And my father? He had the gift of slipping away at the right moment, because he owned the village general store.

"Excuse me Grandma, I've got to go to the shop. If I'm not there the customers hang around gossiping with the salesman, then they're gone without buying anything."

My grandfather, my mother and we children didn't have the same excuse. Especially when it came to the thousand "Hail Marys" on Christmas Eve.

Grandfather, who obstinately insisted on his little glass of whisky which he had sent regularly from Quebec, was more like a good glass of robust red. Ruddy complexioned, bright eyed with broad shoulders and the gift of the gab – the whole village knew his opinion on the Taschereau government which he expounded with a lot of gesticulation and in bad English when the occasion required – he was, nevertheless, incapable of fooling my grandmother. He was like putty in her hands to the extent that, while he would have preferred to be a pillar of the cabaret rather than a pillar of the church, every Sunday morning he was there, with the rest of his family, in the front pew.

The worst day of the year for Grandfather was, without a doubt, Christmas Eve with its thousand "Hail Marys."

I knew that he already had his supply of whisky in the basement and that he would be sure to interrupt the saying of the twenty rosaries (ten in the morning the rest drawn out, come what may, over the afternoon) whenever he felt like taking a trip downstairs. He invariably came back up smelling strongly of mint drops.

The ritual never changed.

Once my father had left like a whirlwind as soon as breakfast was over, my grandfather would pick up his fur coat with one hand and nimbly get into his fur-lined boots. His beaver hat perched on top of his few remaining hairs, he would reach the door in one bound.

I was always amazed that grandfather, who complained about his rheumatism, could suddenly be so agile.

My grandmother would pretend not to notice till the sudden chill made her turn round towards the half open door.

"Haven't you forgotten something, Granddad?"

With one foot out the door, Grandfather could have turned a deaf ear and continued merrily on his way. But he always made the same mistake. He stopped to answer "that pest of a woman."

"What'd I f'rget?" he would ask, with a suspicious air.

"It's Christmas Eve, Granddad," she would reply. "You can't have forgotten."

Grandfather would feign amazement but didn't take anyone in.

"G'd grief! Heavens! It can't be. All Sain's day's har'ly over!"

A little smile, like the Mona Lisa's would flit across Grandma's face.

"Oh yes!" she would retort. "It's surprising how fast time flies. What can you do. That's the way it is. We have to accept the good Lord's will."

Grandfather wouldn't accept defeat. He would come back towards Grandmother, and, with his most charming smile, would proffer what he considered, depending on the circumstances, to be an irrefutable argument.

"Listen, m' dear. Surely y'c'n do w'out me this mornin'. A promised Tom Brown a'd give'm a han' t' shoe 's horse."

He spoke "joual" much to my grandmother's despair – she who made it her duty to speak her mother tongue correctly. My grandfather, on the contrary, didn't hesitate to swallow his syllables, banishing vowels like so many irksome flies.

At other times it would be a meeting of the oldest members of the conservative club – my grandfather remained a "Tory" to his dying day – that he absolutely had to attend. This was highly unlikely at that time of year. Or it was an appointment with the tinsmith who wanted his opinion about some land. In the middle of winter! Once he even pleaded a toothache that was "unbearable." He had to go to the dentist "ri' now" because he "c'dn't put up wi' it any more." And yet he'd had false teeth since time immemorial. For a long time I had believed that he had been born with them.

But he knew he was lost.

He would end up taking off his coat, throwing his beaver hat in a corner and trailing reluctantly off to find his rosary.

In the name of the Father, the Son and the Holy Spirit…
Hail Mary, full of grace…

Kneeling in front of her rocking chair – she wouldn't sit down before the fifth rosary had been said – Grandmother, eyes shut on the outside world, went back in time, back to the eve of the first Christmas. She was there with the ox and the donkey and the shepherds in front of the manger. And she offered up to the Mother of the Christ Child the fervent, deeply rooted prayer of the humble.

Grandfather, kneeling, at least for the first sets, soon began to rub his thighs, and the back and front of his knees. He ended up crouching on his heels.

"H'ly Mary, Mother o' God... Pray f'r us, poor sinners..."

The beads of his rosary clicked between his fingers.

"Glory to the Father, the Son and the Holy Spirit," murmured Grandmother.

Grandfather's "So be it" burst out like a trumpet call. Then a "Thank God, tha's an'ther ten finished!"

The morning went by reasonably well. The afternoon was more difficult. Grandmother, gradually running out of energy, was forced to pass on the baton. My sister and I took over, under her strict supervision. There was no question of Grandfather leading the "Hail Marys": the decades would be rattled off shamelessly.

Since my mother was busy preparing the Christmas Eve meal, she was excused from duty. However, my grandmother had pointed out to her that she couldn't, in all conscience, not join in the responses.

Poor Mother! Her "Holy Mary, Mother of God" often got mixed up with the contents of her recipe book.

And, looking for distractions, I would listen for the "pray for us…Oh, my goodness! what am I doing? It's supposed to be a teaspoon of vanilla…poor sinners…and I was going to put in a whole tablespoonful…" Or other such digressions. But she got to the *So be it* along with us.

My sister, who was two years older than I, well behaved and sensible, as she still is, submitted to Grandmother's demands without protest.

"What's the use of complaining?" she would say when I rebelled loudly, well out of Grandmother's earshot, against a chore that wasn't in the least bit necessary to show you were a good Catholic. "It's easier to accept it than to make a fuss. You won't change anything and you'll upset Mommy."

She would finish by imitating Grandmother's smile, "After all, it's Christmas Eve."

When it was my turn, I made short work of it, my eyes on the pies and doughnuts defrosting on the kitchen dresser. There were also popcorn balls rolled, a few days before, in syrup which had hardened now – my grandmother's speciality – that my sister and I had threaded during the morning. They were waiting in the fruit bowl to be added to the other Christmas tree decorations.

I must, in all honesty, confess that my ever so good and sensible sister had, perhaps less often than I, succumbed to the temptation to break off a bit of these sweet popcorn balls and taste the forbidden fruit.

Among the memories that rose to the surface of my glass of Vouvray on that Christmas Eve in France one picture suddenly popped up. Much to the surprise of my companions, I burst out laughing while tears ran down my cheeks.

Since lunch the rosaries had followed fast on the heels of one another. We had arrived – I was paying strict attention to them – at the last one. In another quarter of an hour the saying of the thousand "Hail Marys" would be over for another year.

We knew it was a point of honour for Grandmother to recite the last "Hail Mary, Mother of God." Aches, pains and sore limbs were all forgotten so that the last rosary would be an offering of joyous prayers – the homage of an old woman, how old I didn't know – to the Virgin who had carried Eternal Life in her body. There was absolutely no doubt that a thread joined Grandmother, who had also known the mystery of creating life, to the One who, every Christmas, gave birth to a human and divine Being.

Grandmother, once again on her knees, was about to start saying the last rosary. Grandfather, who had come back from his visit to the basement, bright-eyed but less steady on his feet, proudly announced that, as patriarch (this was, too say the least, an exaggeration since we were his only family) he had the right to finish the thousand "Hail Marys." Trying to hide her disappointment, Grandmother thought it best to acquiesce. My mother gave Grandfather a suspicious look then went back to making the Yule log.

Nevertheless, Grandmother couldn't help adding, "You won't forget the invocations?"

My grandmother always held a good number of invocations in reserve: Saint Joseph, Saint Anne, Saint Jude, patron saint of hopeless causes, and goodness knows how many others. She had explained to us that she ended her prayers like that to make good anything she might have missed in the course of her daily intercessions. This exasperated Grandfather. He proclaimed loudly that, in his opinion, every prayer should have a clear, clean, ending "without all sorts of dilly dallying."

Since he didn't respond immediately to Grandmother's exhortation she repeated, gently but firmly, "You know the invocations, Saint Joseph, Saint Anne,…"

"Of course," Grandfather interrupted, "Saint Joseph, Saint Anne and all the rest. Don't worry, I won't miss a single one."

Grandmother clasped her hands round her rosary, closed her eyes, and waited.

Grandfather, with unexpected fervour, began the last "Hail Marys."

Holding himself straight, his eyes closed, he might have been taken for a praying effigy come to life from a medieval cathedral. The rosary beads slipped one after the other through his fingers. The decades followed each other, slowly. Grandfather took pains to stop his booming voice from swallowing words, and to respect tradition.

29

And so we reached the final 'Amen.' All that remained were the invocations so dear to Grandmother's heart.

Without hesitating, Grandfather said them one after the other.

"Saint Joseph…"

"Pray for us," replied Grandmother.

"Saint Anne…"

"Pray for us" we chorused in unison.

"Saint Jude…"

And so on till all Grandmother's favourite intercessors had been invoked.

But Grandfather didn't have the least intention of stopping.

"Saint Paul," he said, all of a sudden.

"Pray for us," replied Grandmother.

"Saint Edward," continued Grandfather.

"Saint Lina…"

My mother cast a worried look at us. She turned towards Grandfather who, head bowed and hands clasped, resumed immediately:

"Saint Vincent…"

Then, all at once, he shouted triumphantly:

"Mallaig… Bonnyville… Col' Lake… Pray for us!"

Grandmother started.

"What have you done, you old fool? Have you gone mad?"

Her voice trembled as with tears in her eyes she breathed, "May the Lord forgive us! You've blasphemed."

She fled to her room as fast as her old legs could carry her.

Roused from her meditation, she had just realized that Grandfather, in his desire to be the winner for once, had added to the saints of Paradise, the list of little stations lining the railway that connected our little Northern Alberta town to the city.

Red with pleasure, Grandfather slapped his thighs and laughed his head off, showing his ivory false teeth.

I joined in his laughter, proud of the trick he had dared play on Grandmother.

Our misplaced joy was short lived.

Grandmother had left her bedroom door wide open and her sobs soon reached our ears. Grandfather's laughter died out. He looked uncertainly, sheepishly from one to the other of us, then, his back hunched, he in turn went into the marital bedroom.

The minutes ticked by, long, interminable, heavy with threat. I was ashamed of having laughed, of the pleasure I had taken in seeing Grandfather "win." My mother stared into space. For the first time since the morning, her hands hung idly at her sides.

In fear of the hand of the Almighty who would surely strike us, I went slowly towards the stairs, wondering what I would find up there. Grandmother's sobs were less frequent. I heard her sniffling a bit, there was a stifled hiccup, then Grandfather's rough voice speaking softly, tenderly.

Sitting on the bed, his right arm encircling the waist of his beloved, Grandfather was saying his rosary and reciting the Hail Marys which were answered by a quavering voice.

I understood that the penance he had imposed on himself was erasing his recent moment of irreverence and the pleasure it had given him. That Christmas would be, as always, a holiday filled with laughter and songs.

I tiptoed back downstairs. Outside, snow was falling silently, reverently, adding its arabesques to the gift of prayers Grandfather was dedicating to the Virgin Mary.

The years have gone by and with them Grandfather and Grandmother, and the glass of Vouvray. But when Christmas comes around, in the midst of the songs and laughter, I imagine Grandmother in Heaven in her very own rocking chair, surrounded by little angels – no cherubim and seraphim, a humble old woman with just a touch of mischief in her, wouldn't dare ask too much – reciting the thousand Hail Marys of Christmas Eve. Beside her is Grandfather and, from time to time, a little angel, less well-behaved than the others, secretly slips him a little glass of whisky.

Paul the Pole

Mademoiselle Josette's gaze lingers on the dark silhouettes of the trees. How many winters does she have left? She is well over sixty. Sixty years, forty of them spent in the country schools of Western Canada.

But, if many long years spent teaching in more or less primitive conditions have left marks no therapy can cure, she has no regrets. Between two breaths from her oxygen bottle, she slowly casts her mind back over the past. Back to her first, brand new school, beside the road and the kilometres she had to walk morning and evening, like most of the children.

In spring the burgeoning violets shivered in their nest of grass, the silken petals of the crocuses trembled in the morning breeze.

So much beauty amongst which she fluttered like a bee seeking nourishment.

In June, the young wheat warmed itself in the summer sun, and grew and grew, mocking the winter which was finally bowing out.

The last weeks of June were not without danger. Prairie fires hatched in the heat.

Mademoiselle Josette hasn't forgotten anything. Certainly not the blizzards that all of a sudden blotted out earth and sky, creating snowdrifts where one sank up to one's knees.

Partly as a game and partly out of necessity, she would zigzag from one snowbank to another forgetting about the gnawing pain in her chest. They were waiting for "the teacher" in the new building: Germaine, Jacques, Normand, Paul the Pole, looking out for her, peering into the formless mass that obliterated everything.

Germaine, Jacques, Normand, Paul the Pole and the others arrived soaked, like her, on rainy days. They laughed as they shook themselves around the box stove which made their clothes steam. She shook herself with them, trying to put her hair back into a style worthy of a teacher who had only just got her diploma.

It was that first year which she remembered most often. How she would have liked to be young again along with Germaine, Jacques, Normand and Paul the Pole!

What has become of them? She can see them, hear them. However, deep down she realizes that now plump Germaine is no doubt an imposing matron; eleven year old Jackie with his red hair is now a silver-templed gentleman; Normand, the lad who couldn't keep still for a moment has no doubt settled down after inheriting his father's farm… and that Paul the Pole… What has become of Paul Pokowskovitch who laughed because no-one could pronounce his last name? His classmates had simply renamed him Paul the Pole. She can't quite fit the skinny little kid, whose unruly mop of blond refused to be tamed, into the picture.

Mademoiselle Josette sees him again, sitting quietly at his desk, his reading book more often than not upside down, watching the comings and goings of the teacher. He was fourteen… She was barely eighteen.

Her cough has come back. Her heart, weakened by asthma, won't hold out indefinitely. Only, she would have liked to see, just one more time, the big and little ones from that first year, in the depths of a countryside that the school inspector often forgot. She would have liked… what exactly would she have liked? To relive a thousand moments, sometimes funny, but sadly, at times tragic too. But she mustn't think too much about the latter. About the Tardif brothers carried away by polio. The death of children, lively as quicksilver one day, paralyzed the next.

Mademoiselle Josette leafs through the pages of the past, skipping over the ones that tell of misfortune.

And so she comes to the famous prairie fire… and Paul the Pole. She stops dead there.

A scorching heat had fallen on the countryside that June. Prairie fires ran along the ground. The farmers watched their fields, lit counter fires, but it was impossible to predict the direction for the fire paid no attention to counter fires nor the dirt roads.

It was about two in the afternoon: from the sound of books being hastily closed the fifteen minute recess was about to begin. But on this particular day, there was none of the whispering that usually accompanied this kind of activity. The children seemed worried. Paul the Pole's eyes were glued to the window.

Mademoiselle Josette spoke to him gently:

"What's the matter, Paul?"

"M'zelle… S'Miss," he said…

"You should say Mademoiselle," she chided as she did every day as a matter of duty. "Or else, Miss. You give some terrible twists to the French language and the English one," she finished with a smile.

"Mademoiselle, S'Miss," he continued. The words tumbled over each other in the language that was still half foreign to him. "If the wind turns… The fire is less than a mile from the school, you know…"

Mademoiselle Josette saw the blackish smoke on the horizon, but nothing else to indicate the heat of a fire.

"You're exaggerating," she said. "There's a lot of smoke, but we're not in danger. It's all still far too far away."

To create a diversion, she announced recess.

The whole class except Paul rushed for the door. He alone stayed with Mademoiselle Josette.

36

As if the door had opened of its own accord, two men appeared on the threshold, armed with spades and pickaxes. The black smoke that had been glimpsed on the horizon a few moments before swept into the room.

"There's not a moment to lose," one of them shouted. "Get going, and hold on to each others' hands, you can hardly see a thing."

Mademoiselle Josette realized how right Paul had been. The wind, suddenly changing direction, had sent the fire in the direction of the school.

"Come on," she said, in her calmest voice, "out you go. I'll follow you."

She watched them as they went out quietly, grabbed the last hand, and closed the door.

They stumbled along, one after the other. Saw the fire pass above their heads. Finally found themselves on the other side of the flaming cloud.

Mademoiselle Josette counted the smoke-blackened faces. One child was missing from the headcount.

"Where's Paul?" she cried.

"We don't know. He went back," replied Normand, pointing in the direction of the school.

"Don't move. I'm going to look for him."

She set out at a run towards the school.

Out of breath, her eyes burning from the smoke, the young woman caught sight of a thin silhouette running towards her, clutching something to his chest.

"Is that you, Paul?" she panted.

"Yes… M'zelle…"

She grabbed him by the hand, not noticing that his hair was full of ashes and his face streaked with soot. She dragged him towards the others without looking at the object he was hugging.

"You disobeyed," she scolded angrily. "You could have been trapped by the flames. What did you think you were doing?"

She was shaking him as she would never have dared if she hadn't been so afraid, when he held out the thing he had been holding carefully in his arms.

"I'm sorry, S'Miss, but we couldn't let Haunani burn."

She took the lava paper weight from him. The head of a young Hawaiian girl with an orchid behind her ear, it was a souvenir unearthed in an old antique shop the year she was at Normal School.

The whole class knew Haunani. The little ones loved stroking her black locks, running their fingers down the bridge of her nose to her full lips. There was something spellbinding about her eyes.

Mademoiselle Josette had used her for many a geography lesson.

In the winter, when the cold kept them huddled around the box stove for the midday lunch break, Mademoiselle Josette's voice carried them off into an imaginary world, far removed from the snowy prairies. The heat of the big, cast iron stove reddened their cheeks as if they were in the Polynesian sun. They were trans-ported to tropical lands where, in their imagination, they paraded in multicoloured malos, short skirted sailors subduing the unruly ocean waves with their powerful oars. They never dreamed that there would be a war and that the men who landed on these mysterious Pacific islands would find very different conditions from those Haunani evoked.

The sound of the doorbell banished the past. Who could it be at this hour? She wasn't expecting anyone and her neighbour never came by before the evening.

Lifting the corner of the curtain she glimpsed a well dressed man who was trying to smooth his grey locks ruffled by the wind. As she hesitated about opening the door, he knocked. Two discrete knocks followed by a longer, more insistent one, and she found herself face to face with a stranger who smiled on seeing her.

"Mademoiselle Josette Hurtubise?"

"Yes," she said, intrigued.

He was tall and slim and held himself erect as if he were in uniform.

"What can I do for you?" she asked.

A light of recognition gleamed in the depths of his eyes.

"Don't you recognize me Mademoiselle Hurtubis? It's true, I'm no longer young, S'Miss." And he gave a great shout of laughter.

"Paul! Paul the Pole!"

"Yes, it's really me. Paul! The same Paul the Pole as long ago. Do you remember?"

"I haven't forgotten you Paul Pokowskovitch. You, or Germaine, Jacques, Normand and the others. In fact, I was just wondering what had become of you all."

"Just call me Paul, M'zelle. I'm just Paul, Paul the Pole. And my grey hair is just as unruly as when it was blond," he added, running his hand through the bushy locks that time had done nothing to tame. "Don't stand on formality with me, S'Miss, otherwise I won't have found the young girl fresh out of Normal school who taught me and talked to us about the tropics," he admonished, his face wreathed in smiles.

"Me neither, I've never forgotten you, S'Miss. I always knew I would see you again one day."

"But how…"

"How did I find you today? Well, for once luck was on my side. It was pure chance that I decided to retire to this town on the coast, and chance again that I found out you were living here."

"But, come and sit down. We have to drink to this wonderful reunion."

She, in turn, laughed, forgetting her asthma and oxygen bottle.

Paul noticed it lying on the sofa and realized that the woman he had loved since his early youth was not in the best of health.

"Come on, tell me what's happened since the time…"

"It would take far too long, and, good grief, it'd be a

bit boring."

He hesitated for a moment before continuing.

"I got to know the tropics as a prisoner of war. There weren't any Haunanis in the camps. But I got some comfort from thinking about the Haunani of my childhood. At night I recited the geography lessons around the box stove to myself."

"And it was you who saved Haunani from the fire. Do you remember?"

"Yes, and I remember you shook me like a rag doll that day. You seemed to be so frightened."

"Yes, I was frightened, I was afraid you wouldn't get away from that cloud of flames going over our heads. You were mad to risk your life for a paper weight," she scolded, as a matter of form.

"I have to admit I didn't stop to think. I only had one idea in my head. Haunani couldn't perish in a stupid prairie fire."

He smiled at the memory of the child running through the smoke and flames hugging a lava paper weight to his chest.

"You were mad," she repeated… "But look, over there on the little table, it's Haunani, covered in cracks, she's aged too. I've never been able to part with her. Maybe because she was my lucky charm that first year I taught. She was my talisman on the days when I felt as if I couldn't answer your questions. You counted on me so much to solve everything."

Paul picked up the paper weight and stroked the rough surface of Haunani's face. His index finger rested on a crack near her eyes. He turned his gaze on the face opposite him.

Mademoiselle Josette was lovely, as lovely with her white hair as she had been when he saw her for the first time when he was fourteen. And he had never denied his attachment to her, which had continued since that day long ago. The war had only strengthened his desire to see her again, if only once.

He started talking, as he hadn't talked for a long time.

He told her how he had heard her voice in the midst of the mind-numbing work the prisoners of war were forced to do. That, in the middle of nights punctuated by the sound of swarming insects and polluted by the smells of refuse piled up pretty well everywhere, it was Mademoiselle Josette he saw. She was talking to them, the children, about wonderful islands which knew neither cold nor snow. Where coconut palms swayed in the breeze and pineapples and sugar cane grew like prairie wheat.

One night, in that dreamlike state between sleep and wakefulness, he relived the Christmas concert of his first year in Canada. An outrigger built by Normand's father according to Mademoiselle Josette's instructions, and pulled by six boys dressed in malos, brought Santa Claus with his sack onto the stage. Little Haunanis, wearing green crowns of paper leaves on their heads and, around their necks, long necklaces of orchids, also made of paper, danced.

Their bare arms moving in harmony, conjured up swaying palms or rolling waves. The act was a great success. There were the traditional songs and recitations but, without a doubt, the inclusion of Hawaii in the programme was the highlight of the show. For a few hours a little school, half buried beneath the snow, was the centre of a good, peaceful, happy world.

But the reality of a long ago time quickly gave way to the horrors of the present. The childhood Christmas concert was distorted and wiped out. The outrigger was suddenly transformed into a greyish submarine, the overflowing sack disappeared in the midst of torpedoes that leapt from the monster's belly. Corpses wearing *malos* floated on the fiery sea and, in the hail of explosives, the Haunani's orchids blazed red.

He woke up with a start, his screams of "Happy Christmas," *Mele Kalimaka*, resounding over the camp. But not once was the Hawaiian welcoming *Aloha* to be heard.

Nightmares? Mirages? Visions of prisoners who reminded him of the past, making him even more painfully aware of the present, of this desert of the soul behind barbed wire. He had sworn then that, if ever he got out of that hole, if he one day returned among the living, he would find Mademoiselle Josette.

Years have gone by… the war too is over. And here he is with her. She's not much older than himself, a white-haired woman, with fine lines around her eyes, her oxygen bottle beside her. She smiles… and there she is, the "S'Miss" of long ago.

And Paul the Pole promises himself to come back often and… one day… maybe… he'll not leave again.

House of Lilacs

The old man went down the three steps leading to the patio. His newspaper was waiting for him.

He walked slowly, one hand holding onto the rail. His legs were not as strong as they used to be. But he held his shoulders straight, his head high.

A halo of white hair framed his face, softening his square chin.

He smiled at the sight of the lilacs at the bottom of the garden. A late dew glistened on the clusters of blue tinged violet, like pearls on velvet. The climbing rose had flowered during the night. A riot of red petals cascaded down the wall on the left.

But his gaze rested on the lilacs. He had planted them himself when they were barely a few centimetres high. He had watched them stretch upwards and fill out in the sun till they became these lovely bushes on which hung a multitude of flowers.

Cathy had never asked him why he was so attached to the lilacs. Father and daughter had simply understood each other.

The old house, the house from the past, it had lilacs too. In summer they overflowed onto the front stoop.

The House of Lilacs! That's how it was known in the village.

The old man opened his newspaper.

"Cathy! Cathy! Come here, quick!"

Cathy arrived at a run. Her father had fallen, he had had a heart attack!

She was completely astonished to find him standing, brandishing the newspaper vigorously.

"Good grief, Dad! Do you realize what a fright you gave me?"

She fell into the garden chair, not knowing whether to be angry or to laugh.

"You gave me the fright of my life. I'm quite shaken up." She gave an exasperated sigh.

"What's happened to put you in such a state?"

The old man was not listening to her. His index finger was on the dark letters of the headline.

"Look! D'you see? The village is going to celebrate its 75th anniversary. Next month! Its 75th anniversary! Do you realize?"

He burst out laughing. His convulsive laughter, very close to sobs, expressed such joy that it was painful to hear.

"Seventy five years! It's not possible! Good God, it's not possible! And to think that I saw that village being born. My village."

Cathy felt her throat tighten.

46

"You're exaggerating," she said. "The village was almost ten years old when you arrived."

A smile touched the corners of her lips.

"In any case, what's all that got to do with you now? You left so long ago. We left," she corrected herself with a bitterness she did not try to hide.

The old man shook his head.

"If I didn't see it born, I as good as did," he concluded. "When I arrived it was no more than a little settlement with a sorry little chapel and a shack that served as a school. No road. No railway line."

His voice rose in the morning silence, frightening off the birds that were pecking about around them.

"I saw it grow, my village, our village. I helped it grow, I worked for it for more than twenty five years. And, when we left, it was linked to the city by the railroad. We had a beautiful church with a real bell tower, and a big school for the kids. A gravel road too. Do you remember, Cathy?"

Cathy was overcome by a wave of sudden anger.

"Yes, I also remember that Mother died there…I haven't forgotten anything. Nor have I forgotten why we left what you insist on calling your village in spite of the way you were treated by those who used to be your friends. Call it 'your' village if you like, but it is no longer mine… nor has it been for a long time."

Her father's face darkened as if a cloud had passed over the sun.

"Don't be mean, Cathy. It's not like you to bear a grudge against people."

The smile he gave her was so timid, so much in contrast to her recent brusqueness, that she was ashamed to have let him guess at the bitterness she still felt towards the village she had grown up in. Where there had been Lucien... before that business.

She leaned quickly over the old man to tidy the strands of white hair that were threatening to fly away with the morning breeze.

"Me neither, Cathy, I haven't forgotten anything. But I've forgiven. Time heals a lot of things, you know. With age comes understanding, we become a little more tolerant... In the long run, we forgive because we can't be sure that, if we had been in their place, we wouldn't have done the same thing."

Cathy did not reply.

Her shoulders bowed as a sudden feeling of weariness overcame her.

What was the point of going back over the humiliation she had been subjected to? Her father had also suffered. After the trial, her mother's sudden death when Cathy had just turned sixteen. Their hurried departure with no one to shake their hands, say goodbye or wish them luck.

As for Lucien, he had crossed the road to avoid talking to her.

The Depression had disrupted the life of the village, had turned everything upside down. It had destroyed friendships, released the stench of jealousy that festered in the depths of people's consciousness.

The smell of fear clung to one's skin.

Ill fortune had to be warded off! The scourge had to be diverted, expiated if necessary. But what were they to expiate? Their naive optimism? They had fearlessly scattered their seeds at random, and now their foolish hopes were being choked by poisonous weeds.

A scapegoat, a whipping boy who could be blamed for their too easily acquired happiness, their rash presumption, a victim to be sacrificed to the gods of progress and prosperity.

Her father, a labourer on the New Westminster building sites along with his two sons, until the war carried off Paul. This second loss turned his hair white and engraved new lines on his face.

His obstinacy and tenacity kept him going. He continued steadfastly, only he was more pensive, quieter. For twenty years, he and Jacques had toiled, scrimped and saved till between them they had built up the little corner shop bought in 1945 till it took on the shape of a supermarket. When he reached retirement age, he turned the business over to his son and settled with Cathy, now a widow, in this house not far from the sea. And he had planted his lilacs.

They lived comfortably. She had her children and grandchildren. Martha was expecting her third. Her grandfather had decreed it would be a girl. He had been waiting forever for his first great granddaughter. She would be called Paulette, the diminutive for his own name, Paul Deschamps. There was no question of departing from tradition. The names Paul and Paulette had been passed down from generation to generation since the arrival of the first Paul Deschamps in New France.

Cathy sat with her hands quietly in her lap, holding on to the present to prevent the past from resurfacing in her life. To keep from blaming herself for encouraging her father to subscribe to this newspaper where, week after week, he looked for the old names, old friends' names, streets, buildings which were so many markers in the old man's memories.

Cathy, who was kept up to date with what was going on there on the other side of the mountains, had quickly understood that the growth of the village which her father dwelt on, the modernisation he described to her in such detail, only made sense in the context of the place he had known long ago. His reality, his only reality was the village as it was at its beginnings. The rest was merely an unimportant stage set, a theatre decor that could be quickly taken down.

He never talked about the House of Lilacs, the house from the old days. Nor did he mention the young woman who had died there.

The old man's voice interrupted her daydream.

"You know, Cathy, I think I'll go… Yes, I'll go," he declared firmly.

It was clear from the wave of colour that spread to his whitened temples, from his hands crumpling the pages of the newspaper as he skipped lines to read more quickly, that his decision, although sudden, was nonetheless irrevocable. Nothing, neither his age, nor the long tiring journey would persuade her father to change his mind.

"Go where, Dad?"

The contrived lightness in Cathy's voice after the angry outburst of a few moments earlier should have alerted the old man.

But he had already forgotten it. The only thing that mattered was the newspaper he was holding, this glimmer of light from a distant past, a past which he had believed was gone forever. It swallowed up the years of exile as if he had never had to leave the Prairie village. The village he revisited in the evenings as he smoked his pipe, that he found again in his dreams at night.

"Go back there of course, see what's happening, find my old friends again."

"Friends?" Cathy repeated mechanically. "What friends?"

The old man did not hear her.

"It says here," he continued, "that all the old villagers are invited. There's going to be a festival in their honour…in recognition of all they've done for the village. Look," he insisted, "there it is in black and white 'the services they have rendered…'"

His face, still wrinkled with sleep, shone.

"The organizers are sending an invitation to everyone. Mine will arrive soon. I'm one of the oldest along with Félix Laramée, Tom Roy and Jim Johnson."

And, pulling himself up to his full height, "I'm in my eighties," he declared. "Eighty five years old, that should count for something. As for 'the services rendered' well, they don't have far to look. There were plenty of them!

And, if they forget any, I'll soon remind them."

His laugh rang out again. This time he sounded as mischievous as a child planning to play a trick.

"The newspaper has my address. As soon as I have the letter in my hands, I'm off."

And he challenged Cathy with a look.

She was careful not to argue.

"Who's organizing the festival?"

"Lucien Laramée. Felix's boy. Do you remember him?"

From a long way off, the face of a boy barely older than herself, half buried under the patina of the years, surfaced. Burst painfully from the depths of her memory.

"He was your boyfriend. You were always together. To the extent that your mother worried about it. You can't have forgotten him. We called him 'Little Lou.' He was small and skinny but he had a good head on him. He picked up everything. Brighter than all the others. Surely you remember him." He smiled roguishly and hurriedly returned to his newspaper.

Lucien! Little Lou! You were hardly any taller than I was. How I loved you! You never knew it. And you didn't want anything to do with me...after that business. You started seeing that stuck up Gisele, with her holier than thou airs and "keep your hands off me" looks. You, who could never stand her...I would have given you anything. Only, you didn't want anything more to do with me...

Bitterness rose in her, the desire for revenge, to

humiliate them all, just as they had humiliated her. As they had humiliated her father and mother.

Go back to the House of Lilacs? Go back to when she was sixteen?

She shook her head. Time had taken everything except the glimpse of two children on the brink of discovering life who had sought each other with shining eyes and awkward gestures.

It was Little Lou who had given her her pet name, that wonderful night at the end of June. The name she still answered to at fifty.

They had been alone in the old house. Her parents had gone out, then her big brothers. Sitting on the couch with their books on their knees, they were diligently reviewing for the end of year exams. Tired out by hours of painstaking memorization, they had gone out for a breath of air. They sat down on the soft grass – to watch the light fade, the sliver of crescent moon rise in the firmament. The scent of the lilacs touched them gently, that slightly intoxicating fragrance which the first blooms of the season exuded every year. Little Lou's face glowed white in the evening light. His dark eyes gazed at her – turned her into a statue of soft wax that a man's hand, a child-man, could mould as he pleased.

His gaze lingered on her. Mesmerized, she awaited the inevitable. Was consumed with burning desire, hunger, thirst.

After what seemed like an eternity to her, he bent towards her, kissed her on the cheek. In a single movement, she did not know if it was she or Lucien, she was in his arms, her lips pressed against Little Lou's. She was stretched out on the grass which tickled her bare legs, Lucien had popped a button on her white blouse, plunged his damp, warm hand under it and finally discovered the softness of her little pointed breasts. She lay without moving, happy to listen to the child-man moan "Cathy! Cathy!" waiting for release. Floating weightless, light as a feather.

The voice of her neighbour, who was also watching the moon rise, brought them back to reality. Awkwardly, Little Lou helped her up. They parted hastily. Lucien forgot his books on the couch.

She had her work cut out the next day explaining why they were there.

Two weeks later, disaster struck. Little Lou never came back to the House of Lilacs. And, the day before they left, he crossed the road to avoid talking to her.

"I'll be happy to see old Felix again. We got on well together. What stories we told each other! And there was no way to beat him, he won every time. Yes, we were like brothers, Felix and I."

The old man chuckled quietly. He was back in a past before the reversal of their fortunes, before their humiliation and their furtive departure.

Cathy too was contemplating the past.

Like a phantom ship looming out of the mists of time, memories of Little Lou drifted through her mind. The light that danced in his dark eyes. The gentle touch of his lips. The eager mouth, full-lipped, red against his pale face.

"And Little Lou?"

"Yes, Little Lou, or rather Mister Lucien Laramée, as they say in the paper. There's a Mr. Simons and a Mrs. Onychuk too. Don't know them! Anyway, that's not important. Little Lou and his father will remember me."

Lost in thought, the old man retraced the years that had passed step by step, like a traveller surrounded by a landscape that had once been familiar.

"Felix and I sure got that MP who promised us a gravel road then disappeared as soon as the last vote was counted. When he came back on his rounds just before the next elections, Felix and I were waiting for him, and this time we were determined. We said to him straight out, 'What about the highway you were going to have built? We still haven't seen a sign of it. This time, we don't want any promises, we want a proper document, signed in your best handwriting. Or we'll vote for the other party. Understood?' Yes, we were working for the good of the village, those of us they're calling the 'old timers.'"

Cathy did not even contemplate interrupting her father, he was no longer there with her on the patio.

"And then there was the business of the railway line. That time it was the senator who had to deal with us. For, Felix and I knew a thing or two about politics. There were petitions, we did the rounds of the countryside. Hundreds of people signed – the nuns who had just arrived in the village, the priest and the Protestant minister, and he was always on the other side. Then Felix and I went to Ottawa. And that was that."

He coughed to clear his voice.

"You were too little to remember the welcome we gave the first train with its three carriages. The fanfare, the speeches and so on... What a day it was! That evening the village was out of beer. The Mounties turned a blind eye when we had to resort to old Pete's moonshine."

He rubbed his old hands together and laughed out loud, the pages of the newspaper scattered at his feet. He had a secretive look, as if he alone could see the pictures unfolding beyond the horizon.

Cathy waited, motionless, for his memories to dissolve, for the present to reassert itself.

Like a gathering wave, the flood of memories rolled on.

"And we 'old timers,' it was us who built the big school, with its playing field. We dug the foundations of the new church. And, yes, I remember now, it was Felix who put the first touch of paint on my house. That was before you were born... It should still be standing, that old house," he added after a moment.

He looked critically at the lilacs climbing the hill.

"Yes, my old house, it's bound to be still standing. Good quality lumber. No architect, no contract to sign. And no plywood. I had good strong arms then. Your mother was my builder's helper. She was as courageous as could be. She helped me right up to the day before you were born. She left us far too soon," he ended with a sigh. "I never got over it."

Cathy closed her eyes. Forgotten grief made her eyelids burn.

"She loved lilacs. Do you remember the lovely bushes each side of the front stoop? They must still be there. Lilacs live a long time. The House of Lilacs, do you remember it?"

Cathy nodded.

Had she ever forgotten her childhood home, its fir hedge, its lilacs and all the other flowers that her mother had loved?

But the depression had arrived. The one they called 'The Great Depression'. The bankruptcy, the trial, her mother's death, Lucien's cowardly desertion of her. Her father had fled with his three children, abandoning the House of Lilacs to the creditors, bidding farewell to a newly dug grave.

Cathy, at sixteen, had known, if not despair – the word is too strong for a young girl barely out of her childhood – certainly such intense bitterness that she had sworn on her mother's name never to set foot in that Prairie village again.

And here was her father blowing on the embers, stirring up the cinders. The past was taking shape again, burning brighter with every word he said. Burning her as it had long ago.

"That's settled. I'm going to the party too! Once I've got the invitation in my hands, I'll pack my case. You'll help me won't you? You know, with the plane ticket, the hotel room and all the rest? I think I'm a bit too old to deal with all those details."

He gave her a disarming smile.

"Dad, you aren't serious. At your age, it's a tiring trip even by plane. You'll have to spend the night in Edmonton, take the bus and…" she looked searchingly at her father, "lots of things will have changed in forty years. You'll probably not recognize anything. Stay here quietly with us, there's nothing for you there any more."

"There's nothing more for me… are you sure about that?" he grumbled. "Besides," his voice became soft, persuasive, "there's no question of going back there to live. Those times are past. I know that as well as you do. But I must… I must…"

"Why are you so anxious to return to the village that chased you out?" interrupted Cathy bluntly.

"No one chased me out. I left because…well… because I wanted to make a fresh start, a new life for all four of us, and…it wasn't possible any more there."

He looked down at his tightly clasped hands for a moment.

"I'd like," he continued slowly, "I'd like…to see my old house…see it once more. And, while it's not too late…visit your mother's grave. You can't refuse me that."

It was Cathy's turn to lower her eyes. There was nothing more to be said. Her father would go on his pilgrimage.

But she was not any less worried at the thought of this sudden return to a past that no longer existed.

The bus stopped in front of the Happy Rest Inn. He had arrived.

Mounted on pillars to make room for the under-ground parking lot, the concrete building, with its rows of identical windows, took him back for a moment to the city he had left, was it yesterday or this morning? He could not remember.

It crossed his mind that perhaps Cathy had been right to be so strongly opposed to his making the trip at his age. She had even gone so far as to offer to come with him to keep him from "getting into trouble." But he had refused.

The truth – he could admit it now – was that he wanted to come back alone to what he considered was his country, his true country. What he had wanted to make Cathy believe for years, what he had tried to convince himself of – that nothing in the world would make him exchange the suburb where flowers bloomed at the end of February for the long prairie winters – had only been an illusion. A smoke screen for Cathy. And his eyes had been blinkered by the thought that the country on the other side of the mountains was forbidden to him.

"Age has its reasons that reason…"

The thought hovered in the air, a distorted echo from his youthful studies.

He came back to Cathy.

She had had to give in. But, good daughter that she was, she had done everything to make his trip easier. She had reserved a room for him in the best hotel, the Happy Rest Inn, he thought with a grimace in the direction of the portico with its potted palms. Made sure he had his travellers cheques, the return half of his plane ticket and the bus timetable. She had made him promise to phone as soon as he got there.

Cathy's advice was soon forgotten at the sight of a blue sky the like of which does not exist anywhere else in Canada, a sun so bright that the snow is a river of diamonds, the fields spangled with gold in summer.

For weeks, in the smoke wafting up from his pipe in the evenings, he had seen and walked the streets from the old days. He had rebuilt the House of Lilacs. Two storeys: the living room, dining room, four bedrooms, the big kitchen, the fireplace where real logs burned (not those pressed sawdust Press-to-logs) in what his wife had called the family room, long before the words became fashionable. And the lilacs in their place on either side of the stoop.

No television, no stereo, just a modest radio. And a piano around which the family gathered on Sundays.

Those had been the good times… But then there had been the thirties.

He had got on the plane gallantly, carrying his little suitcase, his back as straight as when he was twenty, forgetting for the moment that the much-awaited letter had never arrived.

"It must have got lost somewhere," he had hastened to explain to a sceptical Cathy. "With today's post a letter could easily go as far as Japan by mistake. I'm going anyway. They'll be sure to know me when I get there."

But he got more and more nervous with each post.

Finally, it had all been for the best! He was well and truly in his village. But he did not have the least recollection of the Happy Rest Inn.

He rubbed his face. Feeling the stubble he remembered that he had hardly had time to shave that morning. He had forgotten what time the bus left, he couldn't find the piece of paper where Cathy had written all the information she thought he would need.

His annoyance at the thought that his poor shave and rumpled clothes must make him look a sorry spectacle to the bellboy, who had taken his case, was transferred to the ultra modern hotel. Darn it all! He had not come so far to find himself back in the atmosphere of a big city. What he needed was the old hotel, the Hotel Roy named after its proprietor, Tom Roy, who lived on the second floor. A modest room, running water, yes, but not necessarily. There had been no running water in the village in 1930.

And a good feather bed, soft and cosy, that you sank into knowing your dreams too would be soft and soothing.

There would be no Happy Rest Inn for him! He would sleep at the Hotel Roy tonight.

He took his suitcase out of the hands of a dumbfounded bellboy and turned on his heel.

An hour later he was back. The Hotel Roy no longer existed.

"There's no hotel of that name around here," they said at the garages, the post office and the Tourist Office where an impertinent young whippersnapper declared with supreme indifference, "Roy? Did you say Roy? I guess he moved away like so many of them. He's probably dead by now."

The old man left, slamming the door behind him.

Tom Roy, dead? Before eighty? People didn't die before they were eighty. Not when they had lived an honest life, paid their dues and sometimes more. Even if they were a little too fond of their beer.

The old man burst out laughing, stopping dead in front of the door as the memory of a midnight mass the like of which the village had never seen came back to him.

Apart from his hotelier's ability to turn a blind eye if people did not pay their bill at once, Tom had a magnificent tenor voice. He was at all the parties and weddings as well as the funerals.

That Christmas Eve – it must have been in 1928 – Tom had arrived rather late at the church. Since the honour of singing the traditional "Silent Night" fell to him, the midnight mass was soon going to be the half-past-midnight mass. The priest stood in front of the sanctuary, fiddling nervously with his chasuble. Behind the big cross, the choirboys elbowed each other. A discreet whisper passing from one pew to the next soon became a wave of protest as heads turned as if on a pivot first toward the priest then toward the organ loft. The minutes went by. The church door remained closed.

Tom finally appeared, flanked by two pals who were trying to get him to walk straight, as they propelled him up to the rood screen. Just when no one expected it,

Tom's voice soared like an arrow to the vault, then hung suspended in the joists before cascading back down to the congregation. Everything he had picked up here and there over the years about music burst forth: crescendo and diminuendo, fortissimo, pianissimo, largo and addagio. The priest, hands clasped before the altar, begged his God to stop the masquerade. The indignant faithful were starting to file down the aisles when a last resounding "Kneel!" sent them rushing back to the prayer stools.

The village did not hold a grudge against him for long, not even the priest who trembled at the thought of the affront to his church. Tom knew his men. A few bottles of a good French vintage, God alone knows how he got hold of them, were delivered in secret to the presbytery, and no more mention was made of the strange arrival of the Infant Jesus in 1928 – one of the last years that the village could have been said to be really happy.

The old man went up to his room as soon as dinner was over. He did not treat himself to the small whisky he had promised himself on the first night of his homecoming, in his village.

The flickering light from the red candles in the semidarkness of the bar seemed sinister to him; the rock and roll, the music of the damned.

He ate half-heartedly, too busy searching the room, hoping to catch sight of a face, no doubt wrinkled with age, or a head, probably bald by now, someone who would smile at him. He did not recognize a soul and no one paid any attention to the stranger alone at his table.

Demoralized, he took refuge in his room. That immense room with its red carpet and matching red curtains, the television set opposite the bed, a bed which would certainly not be as soft and comforting as a feather bed. He collapsed onto it, completely exhausted. Waited for the sleep that would not come.

Behind his eyelids, heavy with fatigue, the day's events swirled around like a never-ending dance. The rush by taxi to the bus station. The hours on the highway, his eyes searching the horizon for a landmark, a field, a farm that reflected his memories. But he had finally had to face facts. This road was paved like a city street, it did not follow the old road but had been rebuilt in a straight line connecting A to B to C. There were no more unexpected detours, no more impromptu drives across the prairie. It was flat, geometric, uninteresting. And the countryside faded into insignificance against the television antennae, the big cars in front of the houses.

He had the sudden impression that he was a ghost in the middle of a countryside that made no sense, awoke no echoes.

He felt a sudden, shooting pain in his neck. No matter how he twisted and turned in his bed, trying to burrow into the foam pillow his head just bounced off it. He, who had never known the torment of sleeplessness, lay wide awake.

In despair, cursing the comfortless luxury of the Happy Rest Inn, he turned on his bedside light. He picked up his pipe, filled it and took a long pull of its comforting smoke.

Everything would be better tomorrow. Tomorrow he would find Felix Laramée. And Tom Roy. People didn't die before eighty!

Tomorrow he would see his old house again. The lilacs would be in flower. From there he would go to the cemetery. Then it would be his friends' turn.

He fell asleep at peace with himself, forgetting that he had waited in vain for an invitation that never arrived. Forgetting also that he had promised to phone Cathy.

'Seventy-five years of progress!' proclaimed the poster. 'The town welcomes the old residents and thanks them.'

"Excuse me, Miss. Would you be so kind as to tell me which of the old residents" pointing at the poster, "have booked a room in your hotel?"

The receptionist gave him a suspicious look.

"You see, I'm one of the old timers. I used to live here, and…"

"Uh huh?"

The woman went back to the papers spread out in front of her.

"I would like," the old man hesitated. "I would like…if possible…"

"The Happy Rest Inn is not in the habit of giving out the names of its clients," she replied curtly. "You had better ask at the Tourist Office."

As he headed for the door, the old man thought to himself that Tom Roy would not have behaved like that. He would have been proud to name his clients, and offer them the occasional beer. Tom Roy cared about his reputation.

He was on the point of going out when he caught sight of a pile of books and a photo album on a table

He cast a glance at the reception desk but since the woman, whose suit, the colour of old roses, suddenly seemed to hug her figure a bit too closely, was busy on the telephone, he picked up the album and started scrutinising the photographs.

The faded colours and haziness of some of them gave away not only their age but also the photographer's inexperience. Nevertheless, he recognised Jim Johnson's big belly beneath his white apron. He had been the first butcher to set up shop in the village. And Marc Côté, blacksmith and horse dealer. And Jean Letourneur, the baker. Martine loved his pastries. Right up to the end, even when he was reduced to counting every penny, he bought them for her and the children. Cream puffs, chocolate eclairs, apple turnovers.

That had been in the good old days.

He took out his handkerchief to wipe away what was suspiciously like a tear.

The women wore long dresses that dated from before the twenties. Later, their hair bobbed, they were dressed in short flapper dresses that barely reached their knees.

His wife had refused to have her hair cut. He loved her brown tresses spread over the pillow, wound them around his fingers, making a necklace for the two of them. Or he undid her braids, slowly, tenderly until there was a mass of soft, fine hair in which he would bury his face.

It was the time for love. He had never wanted to know any other.

The men seemed stiff in their Sunday suits. The beaver hats and astrakhan muffs were dark shadows against the snow.

The old man looked at them and chuckled softly. Oh, yes, it was definitely them, they were the young ones then, today they were the old timers, his friends, the people who had been his family, his big village family.

The big family had dissolved without warning, its members withdrawing into themselves, fearful and suspicious. His best friends, Felix Laramée and Tom Roy, had not even dared come to his defence, had sneaked away, refused to get involved for fear of being dragged in, being implicated in his ruin.

But all that belonged to the bad years.

If misfortune had not fallen on the village, if unemployment had not sown discord, he, Paul Deschamps, owner of the general store, would not have been accused of fraud when he suddenly closed his doors. His fault? His mistake rather? Out of fear of hurting or offending people he had hidden the fact that the debts had been accumulating for two years, that the farmers, to whom he always extended credit till after the harvest, were no longer paying their accounts. A fatal decency. Naivety too. For he had believed that his reputation for honesty and decency would be his best defence, that the villagers would understand and testify in his defence. But Tom and Felix were absent on the day of the trial.

In spite of being found innocent because of the lack of concrete evidence, he was none the less isolated. The shop was handed over to his creditors, the House of Lilacs too. All that was left for him was to start over somewhere else. He had lost everything, his wife, his house, his business and those whom he had believed were his friends.

For his wife had died. An attack of appendicitis, the doctor called in too late – Martine had refused to see him up to the last, knowing they would not be able to pay his bill. Grief and shame had played their part. She had suffered as much as, perhaps more, than he – watching him turned overnight into a criminal, a black sheep to be avoided.

She was at rest in the cemetery at the end of the village, behind the church that he, along with Felix and the others, had helped build. He would go and see her this very day, would bring her some of his lilacs, the lilacs they had planted together so long ago.

He put the photograph album back. Failed to notice that he and his wife were not in any of the photos.

He went and sat on a bench in the square where the war memorial monument was, and began turning the pages of the book he had just bought. *Seventy-Five Years of Progress.* The title of the book repeated the slogan on the poster.

He leafed through the book looking, in spite of himself, for a sign that he and Martine had been there, that they also had been judged fit to be included with the others. He licked his thumb, creasing the pages in his haste to find what could not have been missed out.

Finally, he came upon what he was looking for. The House of Lilacs was there, before his eyes. A whole page had been devoted to it. He was so happy that he did not take the time to stop and read the inscription nor the note that had been added.

The roof with its four steel rods protecting it against lightning. He counted the windows one by one. His wife had made the lace curtains herself (it did not cross his mind that these must have been replaced over the years). The big porch where he and Martine sat together on the rocker in the summer evenings. Close together like newlyweds. And the big front stoop with the lilacs in bloom. It was all there. All he needed to do was find it again.

That was when he saw an odd inscription at the bottom of the page.

His name, Paul Deschamps, was not mentioned. The House of Lilacs was attributed to Lucien Laramée. Had been turned into condominiums.

He jumped to his feet, already headed towards the Reception Centre. He would ask for an explanation. He would fight, if necessary, to make those responsible admit that it was his house, the house he had built for his wife and children. He would confront Lucien Laramée, "Little Lou" as he was known in the old days – he would throw every insult he knew in his face. And, if he ran out, he would invent more. No one was going to get away with stealing his house, Martine's house. They would not turn it into an apartment house.

He knew every centimetre of it. His sons, Paul and Jacques' room with all their baseball and hockey paraphernalia, stuffed under the twin beds. Cathy's pink and white room. His and Martine's bedroom, the big bed where they had made love, where the children had been born, where she had died.

He knew that upstairs well with the big staircase leading up to it, the banisters made shiny by the boys, sliding down it every day, in too much of a hurry to take the stairs. And the ground floor. The kitchen, the dining room with its mahogany table, the family room and its fireplace of local stone, then the living room, with its maple wood floor, its piano, its dark red plush covered armchairs. Yes, he knew his house. Their house, Martine's and his house that the depression had carried away with everything else.

The lilacs! They would be in bloom now.

He would go and pick armfuls of them. He would put them on Martine's grave. He certainly owed her that.

The inscription said Munro Street! There had been no Munro Street in his day, his house had been on the main street.

No matter, he would find this Munro Street. Then the people running the Reception Centre would be getting a visit from him. These men who had not even sent him an invitation, who had had the audacity to write Laramée House below its official name. He would teach these devils who had been in too much of a hurry to put some kind of history of the village on sale to check the facts. Either you're a historian or you're not. And there's an end to it!

He walked around the war memorial. He saw the names engraved on the grey stone but refused to stop, sensing that he would not find the name of his older son who had been shot out of the Italian sky in 1944.

He went down one street after another, too proud to ask for directions.

The village had changed completely. Originally laid out like a checker board with the houses lined up along the streets, it now overflowed in all directions, spreading like a monstrous spider's web across what remained of the fields. It caught the tops of skyscrapers in its net, engulfed the tentacle-like arms of shopping centres. Where the children had played soccer in the summer or had made themselves a skating rink in winter, there now stretched an enormous parking lot. No more grass, no more wild flowers.

It was well past noon. His stomach and legs told him so. But he was not a man to abandon a task before seeing it through. No sir! He would keep going to the end, till he reached the house they had stolen from him.

It was there somewhere, on a Munro Street which had once been the village Main Street. He would find it. Then he would leave this village he no longer knew. Cathy was right. You can't relive the past. It is as elusive as the wind flitting through the leaves. We breathe in its freshness for an instant, stretch out our arms to embrace it, and it is no longer there.

Weighed down with sadness, the old man plodded

71

on, slowly, desperately.

All of a sudden it was in front of him.

He stared at it sceptically, then, bracing himself, began examining its every detail. The sign above the front door said House of Lilacs, then underneath: Laramée House. An arrow pointed to the owner's office at the corner of the porch. The house had been covered in some kind of white stucco trimmed with green. But the old man was not mistaken. It was definitely the house from the old days in spite of its modern appearance.

He stood still, taking it in, paying homage to it.

He was filled with joy. A joy he felt would last for the years, months, days that remained to him, that made him forget Cathy and his recent anger. He had done the right thing coming back. This moment was worth the tiring journey, erased the sorrow of learning he was no longer part of his village's history, that his son's name was not engraved on the grey stone, that all that was left for him was a grave in the cemetery.

He crossed the street, stopped at the bottom of the steps.

The lilacs hung in clusters, heavy with early spring fragrance. Were they the same ones that he and his wife had planted and cared for? It didn't matter! He would give Martine her favourite flowers, a last bouquet from him. He would strew her grave with them, pluck the petals one by one till they reached Cathy and her grandchildren.

The festivities? He was no longer thinking about them. He no longer cared if people remembered him.

All the same, murmured a voice deep within him, it would have felt so good to talk about the past, the good years and the bad, to laugh at the tricks they had played on each other. In short, to be welcomed like the traveller who has come home after a long journey.

For that was another reason why he had come back. Cathy had guessed it, repeating on the eve of his departure, "You know, Dad, times have changed a lot. They won't remember anything back there."

"I'm going back to visit your mother's grave. And our old house. Do you understand?"

She had given him a rather sad look and had carried on packing his case.

He stood at the foot of the steps. His eyes were not big enough to take it all in, to absorb it so that it would stay, imprinted on his inner eye.

He no longer saw the obscene red sign pointing to Little Lou's office. Beneath the white and green stucco he saw the brand new wood that he had worked on, cut to size, the raised beams, the plaster with which he and Martine had made the walls.

His gaze fell on the flowering lilacs again.

He was not a botanist. Pistil, stamen, anther, stigma meant nothing to him. But what had always intrigued him was the way the tiny blooms climbed along their stem so that, depending on the angle of the light, they were coloured a dazzling mauve or a lighter, gentler shade at their tip. And their fragrance, light as the first spring breezes with which they conspired to lighten one's heart after the long winter months.

The old man snapped out of his daydream. Approaching the bush on the right, he started picking the clusters of flowers. Then he walked around the stoop to strip the other one.

Using his pocket knife, he cut, carving into the soft wood, collecting one cluster after another, taking his time, for time had ceased to exist.

His arms were soon filled with flowers. Then, and only then did he turn round to continue on his way.

A woman's voice stopped him short.

"What's going on? What do you think you're doing? Stealing from people's houses, in broad daylight now?"

She looked in the direction of the red arrow:

"Lucien! Lucien! Come quick!" she shouted. "There's an old man taking our flowers."

A portly man appeared at the corner of the porch.

"What's going on?" he asked, smoothing the grey lock slicked across his forehead.

"Sir, would you please explain yourself. Your behaviour is, to say the least...out of order."

He spoke in the authoritative voice of a man who has succeeded in life.

"Little Lou," murmured the old man. "Little Lou, is it you? Is it really you?"

"I beg your pardon?"

From his position at the top of the steps, Mr. Laramée looked scornfully at the old man standing below him.

"Is it you, Little Lou? Don't you recognize me?"

"No, sir. I don't know you. And I'm waiting for an

74

explanation…"

"It's…it's me, Paul Deschamps… Don't you remember, Little Lou?… And Cathy? Your girlfriend when you were young? You haven't forgotten her?"

"I am Lucien Laramée, the owner of this house. And I don't know anyone called Cathy. Nor Little Lou. I have no idea who you're talking about."

"He's just been stealing from us and that's all you can find to say to this…this…"

Lucien Laramée gestured at his wife to be quiet.

"Leave it, Gisele," he said. And in a voice that cut through to the bone:

"Why have you damaged our lilacs? It's vandalism! I could have you arrested."

"Little Lou… Lucien… you… you don't recognize me? Paul Deschamps. Your father, Felix's friend. This is my house. I built it with my own hands. You weren't born then."

"What is all this nonsense? You've stolen from us, the proof is there, in your arms. So don't go telling us stories."

And Mrs. Lucien Laramée crossed her arms over her ample bosom.

Distraught, the old man was rooted to the spot.

Could it be that Little Lou didn't recognize him? It was definitely him, nevertheless, in spite of his corpulence and the lock of grey hair hiding his balding head. He had the same dark eyes, a little more narrowed beneath his drooping eyelids. But, in their depths burned a hard, calculating light.

Lucien Laramée burst out laughing.

"That's a good one," he continued. "But, if you're interested," here he looked the stranger who'd arrived from nowhere up and down, "my father, Felix Laramée, is in a nursing home. I've never heard him talk about a… what did you say?… a Paul Deschamps. As for the woman you call 'Cathy' the name means absolutely nothing to me," he added brusquely with a glance at his wife.

He ended coldly:

"But this is all a lot of nonsense and it doesn't compensate me for the loss of my flowers. This house is called the House of Lilacs. That's what it's known for. You can see why! So I expect you to pay me for the flowers you've taken. Come on! Get a move on!"

The old man, clutching the flowers he had stolen, gazed at the couple at the top of the steps

He opened his mouth to try and explain that the House of Lilacs was his, that he and his wife had planted the lilacs. That they had been Martine's favourite flower. But he felt lost before this Little Lou who was no longer Little Lou, and this Gisele who was staring at him like the executioner at his victim.

He would have liked to tell them that they were for Martine's grave. That she had died forty years ago, here, in this very village, during the Great Depression. He wanted to tell them… what exactly? That he had built the House of Lilacs? That they did not have the right to steal it from him in their history of the village? But he had just told them that, and they didn't understand.

"He's an old lunatic," said Gisele Laramée suddenly, breaking the silence that kept all three of them motionless before the devastated bushes. "I've never seen him around here. I don't know where he's come from... But taking our lilacs, really..."

"Call the police," she ordered. "And hurry up before he slips between our fingers."

The policeman arrived at the wheel of a big black motor car.

"Well, well!" he said. "What's happened to you Mr. Laramée?"

Casting a sidelong glance at the armful of flowers which the old man was barely managing to hold on to:

"Is this old man giving you trouble? We'll deal with him then."

The old man suddenly felt guilty.

He no longer knew why he was there except that it was his house and his flowers and that these ones were for his wife. Paralyzed by an inexplicable fear, unable to say a single word to prove that he was not an ordinary thief, nor was he a lunatic escaped from the asylum, he hugged the clusters of lilacs more and more tightly.

In spite of himself, memory took him back to the time of the trial long ago, when everyone had taken him for a criminal.

He began to tremble under the weight of the accusation which was being repeated after so many years.

No, it wasn't possible. You don't have the same nightmare twice.

"They've loaded the dice," he thought.

But who had loaded them? Little Lou? Felix? The village?

"Well, officer," Lucien Laramée began pompously...

"You can see for yourself what's going on, Officer," interrupted Gisele Laramée in a caustic voice. "This old man has robbed us. In broad daylight. While my husband and I were working in the office!"

"He must've thought there was nobody here," she added, with pursed lips.

The policeman turned to the old man. He was rather pathetic with his crushed flowers.

But, as the representative of law and order, he did have to do his duty. He got out his notebook and a ballpoint pen and prepared to ask the usual questions.

"Your name?"

He was going to add "Sir" but, having seen the expression of disdain and anger on Gisele Laramée's face, thought it more prudent not to. It was better to be on the owner's side. It was safer.

"Your name, I said?" he repeated in a stern voice.

"Paul... Paul Deschamps."

"Occupation?"

"I don't have one."

It did not cross his mind to add that he had been retired for many years. That he lived with his daughter, Cathy. This information seemed superfluous. Wasn't it obvious that he had long since reached retirement age?

"Your ID?"

And, as the old man looked uncomprehendingly at him:

"Surely you've got a Social Security card," the policeman said impatiently.

"Yes."

He hastily took his wallet out of the inside pocket of his jacket. No Social Security card. What the devil had he done with it? Cathy had told him to have it with him always.

He fumbled in his wallet. His lips were trembling as were the hands that crumpled the bank notes. But the Social Security card had disappeared.

When had he taken it out of his wallet, and why? And where on earth could he have put it?

As the policeman stood tapping his fingers on his gun holster, the gun ready to use in an instant, realization dawned on the old man.

"It's... It's in my suitcase at the Happy Rest Inn," he said breathlessly.

Mrs. Laramée burst out laughing. The Happy Rest Inn! The best hotel in town! The old man was certainly laying it on thick!

Her husband contented himself with a tight smile that barely lifted the corners of his lips.

The old man said to himself, "That's not Little Lou any more." Little Lou didn't have those thin lips, so thin that they were no more than a thin red line in a flabby face. His mouth had been eager for life, for pleasure. All that remained of Cathy's adolescent friend, was this podgy man with his self-important voice, his thin-lipped mouth. Thank goodness Cathy had not lost any sleep over him! She had found someone much better.

The policeman was writing in his notebook. The old man did not know what he was writing but he sensed it would be used to condemn him. Why did they not leave him in peace with his flowers? They were already beginning to fade.

Where did he come from? Why had he come to the House of Lilacs? And why had he stolen the flowers?

The policeman went calmly on with his questions.

To tell the truth, he was feeling more and more ill at ease in front of this old man who appeared to be disoriented rather than a criminal. Certainly, the fact that he was dealing with an attack on the property of such prominent people as the Laramées, made a definite impression on him. However, this clean-shaven old man in his rumpled clothes, which were clean nonetheless, was not one of those vagrants who came into the neighbourhood to help themselves at the expense of the rich. Perhaps the old man was not quite in possession of his faculties, for who would steal flowers?

He turned to face Lucien Laramée and his wife, standing guard at the top of the steps:

"This poor man looks a bit pale," he said. "Maybe I should take him to the hospital... As for the flowers he took..."

"But he stole them! He stole our lilacs!" shouted Mrs. Laramée. "And what for? Tell me that! Unless it was out of pure spite. And at his age too!"

Stunned by the flood of words, the policeman thought it wise to address her husband:

"Mr. Laramée, you are a respected businessman.

You wouldn't want to cause a scandal in the town, especially not at the moment. A rich man against a poor old man over a few flowers, a mere trifle. It would make a bad impression."

Lucien Laramée gave a faint smile which was closer to a grimace.

"Well, if that's what you think. Maybe we would be better to let it drop…"

"Let it drop! Not on my life! It's theft and that's a crime. Don't matter if it's an old man or a young one, it's the same thing. We're the victims, we have as much right to justice as him."

And, with a swagger, Mrs. Laramée declared proudly, "The rich have the right to it too."

The policeman shrugged his shoulders.

"I still can't arrest some poor man who's a bit touched in the head over a few flowers."

Suddenly he had an idea that might perhaps calm Mrs. Laramée down. ("A bitch of a woman, she's enough to put me off marriage for the rest of my days," he grumbled under his breath.) And it would save him from a ridiculous situation. He could already hear his friends' sniggers. "Hey, here's our Charlie. Taking on old geezers… and flowers now! Congratulations, buddy! You deserve a promotion."

"Would you accept compensation?"

"What kind of compensation?" sniffed Mrs. Laramée. "There's no more lilacs, they'll not grow back before next year."

"Is he going to pay?" asked Lucien Laramée. "Lilacs

are expensive at this time of year."

The policeman had them, the filthy rich. All that remained was to agree on the amount. Judging by the bulging wallet the old man was holding gingerly in his hand he certainly had the inflated amount they would not fail to extract from him.

The old man was not listening any more. He was looking vacantly at the house that had once been his. Then his gaze returned to the clusters of lilac wilting more and more in his arms.

"How much do you want?"

"Officer, I've just told you that lilacs are expensive. They aren't to be found any more. So…"

"Sixty dollars for each bush," his wife snapped. "And not a cent less. You can take it or leave it. If he refuses," (here she did not even deign to look at the old man, standing at the bottom of the steps) "we'll take him to court."

Mr. Laramée, glanced at his wife. His eyes gleaming with disbelief and greed at the thought of making some money.

"A hundred and twenty dollars! For two bushes! That's a bit steep! For flowers that are already wilting."

"You can take it or leave it," repeated Lucien Laramée in turn. "It's only flowers to you. But for us it's the entire reputation of the House of Lilacs, the Laramée House, that's being lost."

The policeman took the wallet, counted out the hundred and twenty dollars and gave them to Mrs. Laramée.

"Right, get going! There's nothing more for you here," he said, turning to the old man.

He raised his voice as much from embarrassment as to prove his authority:

"And, don't even think about doing it again," he added. "For then… you know what to expect."

The old man pulled himself up to his full height. He looked up at the couple. At the top of the steps, they were checking the bundle of notes.

Holding his shoulders straight and his head high, he set out for the cemetery. He did not notice the little faded blue flowers he was scattering behind him, dying in their turn as his village, his wife, and his old house had.

Take My Hands, O Lord!

Softly, I set my foot on the first step. Silently, so as not to frighten away the mysterious call.

There it is, the same door as long ago – I used to love stroking the wood, tracing its grain with my fingertips. Laying my hand flat against its polished surface I would let my fingers glide gently towards the door handle, like a blind man seeking the way in.

But I knew the entranceway well and what it concealed. That profound secret that fulfilled me, when I raised my long, white fingers towards You.

"Take my hands, O Lord! They are Yours."

I dedicated them to worshipping You, pledged them of my own free will, irrevocably, for the rest of my life.

I am looking at these hands. The hands she has always called "your long, white hands," with that rather sly look she has, her mischievous laugh reminding me of what I was, what I have never stopped being. Since my flight so long ago…

I hate them! I hate their deceptive whiteness. I hate

my slender fingertips, my smooth palms on which time has left little trace. My body has shrunk and bent, my muscles have slackened. But my hands have stayed young, as white as on the day I was ordained. Falsely pure. Empty and useless.

"We only see clearly with our hearts," I remember reading much later. Too late to turn back the clock.

However, here I am, back at my point of departure. All I have to do is climb the steps, one by one, turn the brass door handle which gleams like a star in a last ray of sunshine and I will find again the Presence of long ago, calm, constant.

Nevertheless, I left it all one day, swearing that it was over, that I would never again pass through that door. What have I come here for today? To mount the Via Dolorosa of a priesthood that went wrong? How can I know? I am here, waiting... for I don't know what.

How many times have I stopped on the threshold as I am doing now? Cast a last glance, in the late afternoon, at the quiet street bathed in summer heat or streaming with November rain? I would listen to the chirping of birds hidden in the deep foliage, watch the clamorous flight of the gulls towards the freighters in the harbour. Stand spellbound by the starlings wheeling tirelessly in their autumnal rites at dusk. I could never decipher the message of these mad dances beneath a sky that sudden-ly went from glorious luminescence to the delicate mauve of night.

I look along the road again, search the shadows of the chestnut trees. To make sure, reassure myself that she is not there. That she has not followed me. That I am alone, completely alone with this void in the depths of my heart.

She appeared at eleven o'clock mass on Easter Sunday. In the front pew. Her blond hair as smooth as silk. Her face was half hidden by a stubborn lock of hair which gave her a disconcertingly fragile look. The shape of her cheeks gave her the look of a child but there was nothing child-like about her eyes. That mocking smile, which I was to know so well later, was directed at the few daffodils in front of the altar. At the sparse offering, which I had hoped would be so generous, its abundance reflecting each parishioner's effort to decorate the altar.

What naivety, what pride had made me announce from the pulpit three months earlier – for, although I had ruthlessly transformed the inside of the church, I had been careful to respect that pulpit from whose height I held sway over them during my Sunday sermon – that a personal offering of a few daffodils they had grown themselves was worth more in the eyes of Christ the res-urrected than extravagant flower arrangements pur-chased at the florist as they bought butter at the super-market.

I told them they were easy to grow. From the pulpit, I explained how, quoting a gardener I had seen on televi-sion who filled his home with flowers in the depths of winter.

I had not thought at the time that I was striking a

blow at the reputation of the Maison Fioritura. That a considerable portion of its income depended on decorating churches for their various communions. Or, if the thought did cross my mind, I simply paid no attention to it.

The manager arrived like a whirlwind the next morning.

Wearing sandals, jeans and a blue sweater, I was enjoying the early February sunshine that was turning the Japanese flowering cherry in my garden pink. The tree was bathed in a fragrant cloud which engulfed me in scented waves.

I was at peace with the world, a world which, for the moment, had ceased to exist.

The manager had barely got out of his car when he brought me back to the present.

His surly manner was enough to intimidate you while your eye was drawn to his fine wool suit. I noticed that the precise cut compensated for his prematurely rounded shoulders. I smiled as I compared his well-groomed appearance with my casual dress.

"Father, about the... the daffodils, you're not serious are you?"

He was on the attack already. Driving home the point that I did not have the right to deprive businessmen of their rightful earnings.

I sought the words that would calm the wrath that was threatening to descend on me.

"The parish has always had confidence in the

Maison Fioritura. (He was a member, he was even a Knight of Columbus, fourth degree, and his wife was a member of the women's auxiliary.) Father, you wouldn't want to go against an agreement that dates back to my grandfather's arrival in the parish; to the founding of a business which, I admit, had humble beginnings but which has since proved itself. You wouldn't want to break with such an honourable custom, would you?"

His tone of voice and his air of condescension irritated me – he was taking me for a little curate who was still wet behind the ears – I felt like slapping him. I gritted my teeth and said nothing.

"You won't regret ordering from us. Our flower arrangements are superb and our employees are as pretty and friendly as all young girls," here he twisted his mouth into what might have passed for a smile, "and are experts in making up flower baskets. You will be completely satisfied with them. For Easter, we will have a full range of spring flowers: daffodils, narcissus, hyacinths, tulips, freesias, and more besides. You must see our greenhouses, Father. They are a real paradise on earth."

This big man was getting on my nerves, with his travelling salesman's patter. I knew what I wanted and it was not an advertisement for the Maison Fioritura no matter how highly rated it was.

"Besides, your predecessor, the estimable Father Thomas, was highly respected throughout the parish... Oh! The dear man, he left us far too soon, a heart attack you know... Well, we really liked him... There weren't any problems with him. We each did our own thing...

He was one of our best clients. He would never have thought of such… (the word 'ridiculous' hovered on his lips) innovation."

"Mr. Gardiner, I certainly understand your interest in decorating our church for the Easter celebrations." I smiled to myself; for the gleam in his eyes was as much from greed at the thought of making a profit, as from the wish of the devout to decorate the sanctuary. "But we must follow the directives of Vatican II. And it seems to me that…"

His slight paunch strained against his rather tight-fitting suit.

"And a lot of good it's done us! An upheaval that has only upset people. No more Latin, no more Gregorian chants, and a handshake for all and sundry right in the middle of mass. And, on top of all that, pop masses to attract the young apparently. Guitars, accordions, violins, banjos the whole kit and caboodle for a dance-hall orchestra."

"Times have changed, Mr. Gardiner. You must be aware of that. If the Maison Fioritura has grown, it's because it's been able to adapt to new conditions, face up to the competition. That's what the media and television are doing today. Attracting the public, in a word, enticing them. Don't you agree?"

It was my turn to hold forth.

"The participation of the faithful in the mystery of the Resurrection, even if it is only with a few flowers which certainly won't compete with your elegant creations, seems to me to be very much in keeping with the

Holy Father's views. Perhaps what has been sadly lacking in our relationship with God till now is exactly that, the gift of ourselves, the simple offering of something from the heart, instead of money we take out of our pockets willingly or grudgingly."

Mr. Gardiner went red in the face. I had hit the mark. I felt that he would never forgive me. But I did not care. Had I not come to shake this parish out of its contented somnolence? So, it was with a certain indulgence that I continued,

"We have been content to follow the Church's rules to the letter, and we have forgotten the spirit behind it. I would like to put that situation to rights. To the extent that I can, of course."

I added, with a tight smile, "If the parish wants to back up its priest."

"And you propose to gain your parishioners' support with this kind of childishness!"

He had taken up the gauntlet, now it was up to me to defend myself. To tell the truth, I would be only too pleased to pit myself against this fat cat who stank of money.

"Well, sir. Perhaps it is just childishness in your eyes, but did Christ not say that, to enter His Kingdom, we must be as little children? My idea, however preposterous it may seem to you, is a first step towards God. The gesture of a child who slips through the police cordon to present his little bunch of flowers to the Queen."

I looked him straight in the eye.

"Are we not God's children, sir? And is it not time to

throw our doors wide to new winds? The sea breezes only a few steps away from us can only make us feel the call of an infinity that is ever changing and yet always the same. What do you think, Mr. Gardiner."

"You're a poet, Father. Have you never had to dirty your hands?"

His sarcasm rang in my ears. I looked at my hands. He was right. They were not the hands of a man who did manual work. They were white, without calluses, unlined.

I replied curtly, "A poet when I'm in the mood, Mr. Gardiner, when I'm in the mood. But that's not what we are talking about at the moment…"

He interrupted me bluntly.

"You won't change your mind?"

"No."

I was not to see him or his wife at mass again.

My assistant, the old priest whom my superiors had advised me to consult before carrying out any reforms that were too daring, came to me in turn. "You will find his advice very valuable," I had been assured.

In the black cassock that he wore in rain or shine, he came to see me. Undoubtedly he found my predilection for jeans hardly suitable for a priest but he took good care not to mention it.

My interview with the florist shop's manager had left a bitter taste in my mouth and I was annoyed with him for coming at once to play his role of mentor.

The peace I had been enjoying until the arrival of the Maison Fioritura disappeared on the rising wind along with the petals from the barely opened flowers.

"Father, I'm sorry to disturb you but…"

"Yes, yes, I know. You saw Mr. Gardiner's Mercedes. The business of the daffodils is ridiculous, I agree. But we have to start somewhere."

I was so angry my head was pounding.

"I'm not going to get bogged down by the insular habits of the parish big shots. I'm sick and tired of these whitened sepulchres."

"Oh, Father!" whispered my assistant, without sounding too reproachful. "No doubt you are right, but the fact is that Mr. Gardiner is one of our benefactors. He has always been very generous."

"No doubt," I thought, "but his charity also reduces his income taxes." I felt I was being unjust but how does one reconcile God and Mammon? The wealthy middle class who sat in the best pews at Sunday mass, never missing a Sunday, were big business people the rest of the week, counting their money with hardly a thought for the poor who crossed their paths.

My assistant continued, "If Mr. Gardiner harbours, more or less justifiably, a resentment against you, it could influence, wrongly, I admit, but nevertheless influence, a lot of our people."

The old priest was right too. I was to learn this over the next few months.

"I certainly can't change my mind. It would look as if I don't know what I want. That's not what is expected of a priest. Even a young one," I added shrewdly, almost mockingly.

The old assistant reddened. He had a sort of paternal affection for me. He knew my stubbornness was as absurd as the subject of the dispute.

"There is a risk that the parish will split into two camps," he ended unhappily. "Some people are already accusing us of," he stumbled over the words, "creating havoc in the good Lord's church."

He said "we" but he knew I was solely responsible. I had replaced the big silver crucifix with a wooden Christ whose tormented features had been roughly carved by a street sculptor. I had relegated the huge statue of the Virgin to the attic. I had got rid of the cluster of candles before which the matrons murmured their invocations. I had definitively put an end to special funerals for the elite.

Throw all the traditions on the scrap heap! Long live the winds of change!

To convince myself, I repeated, "I carry the sword of justice," as our Lord said. "And it will take a smart man to stop me!"

Which the Lord did not say.

What presumption! How little I understood the message of the Gospel!

I jumped to my feet to make it clear the interview was over, cast a glance at the old man's worn cassock and turned on my heels.

What became of my faithful old friend? What sorrow the coward's flight must have caused him. And what reasons did he invent to avoid scandal?

Naturally, the anticipated innovation fell well short of the mark.

That Easter morning, a morning which promised fine weather, a dozen wilting daffodils, from the old assistant who did not want his priest to be disappointed, were all that dressed the altar.

She was there, turning her gaze on me as my hands lifted the host over an almost empty nave.

I finally turn the door handle. I sink down onto a pew at the back of the church and hide my face in my hands to shut out the little red flame flickering faithfully at its post.

"Take my hands, O Lord!"

Lord, I first gave my hands to you the day I was ordained. I promised my long white hands would serve You for ever.

Only, one day, in despair, I reclaimed them. And I threw away my priesthood as if it were a worn out garment that had been on my back too long. I erased from my memory the refrain I used to repeat quietly to myself simply for the pleasure of knowing You heard it, You accepted it.

"Take my hands, O Lord. They are Yours."

My hands have remained white. The florist was right, I have not dirtied them for anyone.

Not even for Tara.

Tara? She was an excuse, an escape that put an end to the chaos of a ministry that had become a pathetic travesty. The star I steered towards to forget the parish that was going downhill. Tara, my lucky and unlucky star!

I see once again my hair curling around the neck of my chasuble, the tight curls of my ash-blond sideburns. I see myself, as if it were today, in jeans and a turtleneck sweater. Or wearing a sweatshirt like the Flower Children. I was like them, in heart and mind. That is why I became so passionately attached to them. That too must have caused a scandal. As much so as the constant presence of Tara at Sunday mass.

She would settle languidly into the front pew, a smile on her lips and, in the depths of her eyes, a question. Knowing she was there, so close, paying attention to my every gesture, compensated a little for the others, those who had been entrusted to me, as they progressively distanced themselves. I forgot them a little more each day… and finally I was left alone… with Her.

I see myself as I was when I arrived in the parish. Convinced that I carried the truth within me and that they could not fail to trust in me.

But that was not the case. And I got tired of it. I deserted the sheep after abandoning my flock... The Flower Children whom I had seen as my younger brothers continued to live in a drug induced fantasy world, roaming the streets with a vacant stare, lips twisted in a beatific smile, in a state of intoxication I too was to know.

The hands You consecrated have known other gods, they have known a woman... but I could not love her either.

I am here before You again, and I dare not look at You... a cog turning in a void, damned in this life... so much so that I no longer even think about the other... the one I preached about in the past... I withdrew my hands, Lord, and You slipped between my fingers... You have never returned...

"Only the heart sees clearly."

I have no heart, for I was unable to see You or my fellow men. I have never got close to anyone, not my God, not men, not even a woman.

I can hear my old flock.

"It's sacrilege!" exclaimed Mrs. Blanchard.

On that particular Sunday I had naively asserted that Luther had not been entirely in the wrong. That we should try to understand and that the movie playing at the local cinema reflected a truth that was not well known.

"Comin' to mass t'hear the likes of that. Luther! A renegade, a heretic condemned by the Church! It's enough t' make you lose y'r faith."

"I'll accept the Yahwe and 'Shaloms' if he's so keen on the Jews," added Judge Lasnier, "but standing up for Luther…"

"If we want to hear Yahwe and 'Shaloms,' we c'n just go to t' synagogue… At least we'd be with real Jews there… As for Luther, well! that's for the Bishop t'decide. He's gonna have to know what's bin goin' on in the parish for th' last while."

This comment came from the Larocque Real Estate Agency salesman who was making his fortune thanks to an unexpected influx of newcomers. Of course, he chose his language more carefully when he talked to potential clients. However, at the moment, dressed in his pearl grey corduroy jacket and maroon pants he was putting on a show, clapping people on the shoulders, enjoying talking in the vernacular.

"Yes," continued Judge Lasnier in his courtroom voice, "I'm afraid we will have to consider that eventuality."

The corners of his grey moustache twitched as he gave an abrupt laugh. A sound which must have made more than one accused tremble in his boots.

But Mrs. Blanchard had not finished her harangue.

"Have you noticed that Christ with its face all twisted at the back of the sanctuary? Where's our lovely silver crucifix! God knows what's become of it."

She added nastily, "P'rhaps it's fallen into th' hands

of them… them hippies, Flower Children they're called, that he hangs around t' bring them back t' God, or so it seems. As if y' could convert drug addicts that don' b'lieve in God or the Devil."

When he was still new in the parish, and they had not realized the extent of his reforms, some of them came up to shake his hand after mass. Now they kept their distance and their comments did not bode well for the future.

But he stayed there, hands clasped in front of his priest's robes, a knowing smile on his lips.

"You'll see lot's more," he said, to himself, sotto-voce. "The bishops stand up for their priests. All it takes is one good letter from His Excellency and you'll all be back in line at the double."

Summoned to the Bishop's palace, he found it impossible to convince such an experienced politician as His Lordship. No matter how much he stressed that his greatest desire was to renew the spiritual life of the parish, bring it into line with the present world (for was that not Jean XXIII's message?), he did not obtain the support he expected.

"It can't be done overnight," the prelate maintained. "You have to be able to wait… be patient and charitable. You can't rush people. And, above all," pointing his finger as he would at a recalcitrant child, "above all, you have to avoid offending them."

However, there was a look of accusation behind his smile as he added, "You've certainly gone all out if I can believe the reports I've received. A Christ with a tortured expression in the sanctuary, a pop mass with songs that have more in common with street rock and roll than with the praise due to God, not to mention your untimely allusion to Luther and your using 'Shalom' as a benediction! You have to admit that is enough to appal the faithful in a parish that is… let's say… right wing."

"You mean the self-righteous, the whitened sepulchres of the Gospel, Your Lordship. In my opinion, if you will permit me to express an opinion, Your Excellency," his superior frowned at his ironic tone, "there is only one way to deal with them. Force them out into the open. Use violence, if necessary. Did our Saviour not say 'I came not to send peace but a sword'?"

The prelate looked at him long and hard.

"He also said 'Blessed are the merciful for they shall receive mercy.' And Saint Paul tells us, 'Charity suffereth long and is kind.' Take care, my son," he added gently, "you are on the wrong track. Your ambition, if I dare say so, and perhaps even your pride are leading you astray. Back off quietly, at least for the moment. Your parishioners will easily forgive your excessive zeal. They will blame it on your youth. I advise you," here his voice became more severe, "to arrange a meeting with Mr. Gardiner and Judge Lasnier immediately. Come to an understanding… and put the Shaloms and Negro spirituals aside for the moment."

Nevertheless, he made one last attempt.

"There are the others, Your Lordship."

"The others?"

"Yes. The lost sheep of the Gospel. Or rather the lost

lambs. The ones hanging around the streets looking for something but not knowing what it is they are looking for."

"Ah yes! Them! I have also been told that you spend a good part of your days with that band of young loiterers; layabouts from what people say. Apparently there is even a young girl who is causing a scandal at Sunday mass. And you are encouraging her."

It was at that moment that the seed of heresy was sown. It was to spread its roots, stifle his ministry a little more each day, and finally choke off any desire to serve God and his parish.

I fled, the weakest of the weak. I turned my back on You, Lord. The only person I wanted to see was Tara.

Nevertheless, my hands have always sought You. In the streets of all the cities I have lived in with Tara, in the middle of nights spent lying beside her, they reached out towards You, You who no longer wanted them.

I can barely see the little flame before your tabernacle; everything else has melted into a darkness as impervious as the darkness within me.

Tell me, Lord, what must I do with these long, white hands that I dedicated to You so long ago?

* * *

There you are! You've come back to your church like a murderer to the scene of his crime.

Crouching in the corner of "your" confessional, you don't see me, my blond hair... I followed you at a distance, discreetly, but never really losing sight of you, taking detours among the streets and avenues and always finding you again, a hundred paces ahead of me, walking straight on, your whole body, your beautiful body, older, a little shrunken, but I still love it, pulled along by that invisible thread that you have never let go of, or that you didn't want to let go... Your hands dangling at your sides... As if I didn't know where you were going... as if the false gaiety of your laugh this morning could have fooled me... All day you've been like a little boy trying to look innocent as he plans some mischief; with your sidelong glances over the top of your glasses. Those glasses that are always about to slip down onto your nose. That too short nose... I laughed at it the first time at that Easter Sunday mass. Later I loved that little turned up nose that made you look like a big kid in spite of your authoritarian air and your learned words...

However, you didn't fool me. Your excuses and explanations were no use. I had guessed – it was pretty easy – why it was so important for you to come back to this city. You talked and talked... you, who are usually so uncommunicative. But you refused to admit that you couldn't go on living with me, trailing from one city to the next, that you'd have sent me to the Devil if you could have... And me, I've been crazy about you since that first Sunday, I'm not about to let you go... Anyway, you could have dropped me if you'd wanted to… I wasn't always with you… In fact, you never asked where we found the money we needed to travel or just to live. You never asked any questions about what I did on my long afternoons and evenings. You took… and you took… without even a thank you.

You were homely, you know. But I loved you. I've loved you ever since that first mass with your sad-looking daffodils. Only you've never loved me…

I admit I must have looked pretty repulsive to you. Dressed like a scarecrow with my gaudy old skirt drooping around my calves. I wasn't a very tempting sight. It was your fault too. When you were kind to me and took the trouble to see me, Tara, and not just some woman, I tidied myself up a bit. To make you forget. Forget what? I didn't know. It was for you. You would smile and caress me and suddenly your eyes would cloud over. It was as if you were looking for something within yourself, outside of you? How could I have known? You would refuse to answer or you'd get angry. Tell me it was none of my business… That I was not your wife – hardly even your mistress. You were searching… you searched for ten years. Oh! Not for another woman. I was quite enough for you on that score.

There was always someone between us, a sort of Presence that you were afraid of but couldn't or wouldn't drive away. How do I know all this? I've not lived with you all these years, moving from one town to another, without getting to know you. My feminine intuition, if you like, or a touch of maternal feeling in the midst of passion! Whether you want to admit it or not, we've had our moments. And, my God, what moments! It was enough to make you lose yourself. Only, you never did entirely. The unknown Presence came between our bodies, separating us once more. You turned over to face the wall, you abandoned me as brutally as you had taken me. Then I turned my back on you too, leaving you to the Presence. It always won.

Do you remember your famous Easter Sunday with its ridiculous daffodils? It was the first time I had entered a church. It had to be yours! I slumped down on the seat just in front of the altar. I was curious and intrigued by what I later called your high and mighty airs. I still don't understand them and you never wanted to explain anything to me. But I liked watching your gestures, the way you moved your hands. I resent them. They belong to that Presence that stopped you from loving me. Do you remember? I was about to light a cigarette and you gave me one of those looks! I didn't dare... I've always been afraid of those looks. That's another reason why I've never asked you too many questions. Anyway, I knew you would never answer them.

Do you remember? You talked about love. Oh! Not the "love" (if I can call it love) that we knew later, but the love of a brother for his brother, of a neighbour for his neighbour. I didn't understand much of it, especially when you talked about the one you called "The risen Christ." Nevertheless, listening to you I felt that, no matter how much we laughed at religion, your words expressed a beautiful sentiment. And I was ready to believe it, especially when your beautiful white hands tried to bring all your parishioners, and me, into their embrace.

Coming out of the church I heard those you had just called "my dear brothers, my dear sisters" ridiculing your words in the same way as they had laughed at your daffodils. I felt sorry for you, you'd spoken with such conviction. And I came back to your church every Sunday till the day when… yes, till the day when, after mass, you took off your white vestment with its gold cross, went out a side door, and followed me.

I took you to my place. You seemed so unhappy that I poured you a big glass of whisky. You drank it in one gulp. Then you started laughing… great shouts of laughter which suddenly stopped as if you were about to start crying… I didn't say anything. What could I have said? I didn't understand, but I was angry with your parishioners, these people you called "my dear brothers, my dear sisters," who laughed at you behind your back. You fell asleep. Your throat was choked with sobs. I could see them as they swelled, straining against the sinews of your neck. It was like a storm raging in your throat. You slept till evening. You didn't even notice that a guy had come by. We spoke in a whisper, he gave me a little package, and I sent him away quickly.

We ate, we drank some more and I offered you a joint. I was sure you would refuse but you threw yourself on it like a drowning man clutching at a straw.

Drowning? Maybe that's what you were. You didn't go home that night, nor on the days that followed. You stayed in the bedroom for a whole week, racking your brains, your head in your hands, your beautiful white hands that I loved, that I still love, like everything about you. You didn't see me, you didn't even look at me, but I knew you needed someone. I looked after you, served your meals, tidied your room. And I slept on the couch. And then, one day, we left the city, your city, and your parish and started our life together.

Do you remember Puerto Vallarta? We arrived there one December evening. I had been afraid at the border. You didn't know, you followed me like a little sheep. But I had drugs hidden in the lining of the suitcase. You might have thought the customs officer suspected something.

"Open your case, Miss," he said to me. "And show me your passports."

He took his time examining everything. But the drugs were so well hidden in a sort of false bottom that he couldn't find anything. We were searched. I was already picturing us in prison. In the end, it was you that saved the day. You seemed so unaccustomed to all the to-do – a customs officer here, another there, and, in addition, a policeman – that the one in charge shrugged his shoulders and let us through. I felt that same suspicious look boring into my back. But you didn't notice anything. You even seemed surprised that you had been searched. Maybe you thought it was the custom.

Naturally, I wasn't so stupid as to tell you why; you would have been quite capable of giving up the package.

Puerto Vallarta was also where you got angrier with me than you ever had before.

There was that church near the centre of the town. I don't know why, but it appealed to me. Maybe because it reminded me of your church. Oh! Not because of its architecture, it was much more imposing than yours. Maybe it was because I hoped to find the answer to the riddle, discover the secret that stopped you from being completely mine. That Presence that possessed you through and through!

You were walking beside me, not saying a word, looking at the children in the street. Did you see them? I wonder. Or were you seeing others you had known? You stopped in front of the market. You listened to the hawkers' patter as they stood in front of their stalls. You slipped a few pesos into the hand of a kid selling newspapers, but you forgot to take the paper he was holding out to you so that the *muchacho* ran after us to give it to you. You shoved it into your pocket with an indifferent *gracias*. I should have realized that it was hardly the time to visit a church. But I refused to be stopped by what I thought was just another of your moods and we walked on up the street towards the Church of the Madonna.

Oh, that was quite the temper tantrum. You can be proud of it!

"What are we doing here?" you shouted.

Your face had gone as red as the bougainvillaea that

cascaded down the little wall beside us.

"You little fool! You've still not understood that all that's finished, finished, finished!"

You weren't just shouting, you were howling with rage. So loud that the women on the church steps turned round to look at us.

You raised your hand to slap me. That was when one of the Mexican women came and stood between us. She looked you in the eye and said, very quietly, "*Por qué?*"

I didn't move. I was waiting for the sting of your fingers on my cheek. But you lowered your hand, and turned down the first street you came to. I didn't see you again for the rest of the day.

Why tell you that I sat down on one of the steps and cried my heart out?

You didn't like the sea either. Why? Because it reminded you of the sea from the past? You never said and I never asked. What would have been the point? You were with me, that's all I asked. And when you seemed in too much despair there was always marijuana. Today I wonder if you really knew what you were smoking, if you wanted to know. Probably not. No more than you wanted to know why we were always packing our bags.

We came back to the Canadian Prairies. You looked for work. But, my poor darling, what else did you know apart from the priesthood even though you were no longer a priest. When you tried to get hired in the oil industry, they laughed at your white hands. They gave them odd looks as if they suspected something. One worker asked you jokingly how you had managed to keep them so clean up to then.

"You sure haven't been doing heavy work," was what he said. "You've sure never worked with oil and grease, man. Or done heavy construction work. D'you at least know what a beam is, or a corner brace? And a derrick, a pipe-line, do they mean anything to you?"

You didn't answer, and I pretended I hadn't heard anything.

One fine day we arrived in Marrakesh. I was trafficking heroin by then. Not for myself, of course, but for an Arab dealer I had met in New York. We had to live after all. You never knew anything about it and I never offered you any. Sure, as much pot as you wanted. But nothing else. Something, maybe the Presence stopped me.

You liked Marrakesh's streets, lined with orange trees; its souks where everything was mixed up together: from carpets, copper and snake charmers down to the so-called dentist who wanted, at all costs, to fix two gold incisors in your mouth. At the cheapest price, he insisted. Do you remember? It's the only time I saw you laugh, I mean, really laugh, like a child laughing at the absurdities of adults.

No, I'm wrong! You laughed at the old Arab at the

hotel too when he called you 'Sir' and, in the next breath, called you 'buddy'.

He would sit for hours in a corner of the corridor, basking in the heat of the sun. Fingering the beads of what looked like a sort of rosary. You never looked at it. If, by chance, you caught sight of the big beads between his fingers, you looked away quickly. But I knew you hid a rosary at the bottom of the suitcase like I hid my pouches of heroin.

Yes, you liked Abdul. He belonged to another environment, another race. He couldn't remind you of your old life. Whereas I...

But all that belongs to the past like London, Paris, Amsterdam...

We are back again in your church. *Maktub heik!* It was written, as the Arabs say.

I can see you quite clearly from where I am: your stooped back, your shoulders sagging beneath I don't know what burden. I follow the movement of your hands. You are looking at them is if they are no longer part of you.

These are no longer the hands I clasped in mine, often against your will. No longer the hands that caressed my body then pushed me away as if I was a demon. Oh, I loved you, but I hated you too: I don't know if I still love you or if hate has become stronger than love. How can I tell? Aren't they both related in some way? But you won't escape. You are mine, d'you hear, I won't let anyone take you, not even that Presence that has spoilt everything.

Ah, now you're lifting your head up. And you are reaching out your hands, palms outstretched, to the tiny flickering flame. They are a white patch in the darkness. The sun, no doubt, has disappeared behind the mountains. The dim light from the windows scarcely cuts through the darkness rising around us.

I leave this stall at the back of *your* church and tiptoe quietly forward. You don't hear anything, you're too engrossed in the little red flame. Do you think it is going to answer you? You clasp your hands. They fall back as if they are tired of waiting for a reply that doesn't come. Look at you there on your knees. Are you asking to be forgiven? Asking the Presence? If that's why you've come back you're wasting your time, there's nothing more for you here. Nothing except a red and gold rectangular box with a white cloth in front of it where I can barely make out the design, a basket of bread and two fishes, on it. You never wanted to tell me what those fish were doing there… I'd have liked to know, to understand… Maybe then that Presence would have meant something to me. What do you expect? I don't know anything about your religion except that you still belong to it or the Presence.

Do you remember. You threw it all away, ten years ago. D'you think your Presence has forgotten that? You can't turn the clock back, it's too late, much too late. There's nothing left for you here.

And besides, you are mine, d'you hear. Tara, who you called your "lucky" star or your "unlucky" one depending on your mood or whim. Depending on whether you wanted me for yourself for a moment, or damned me to Hell.

Well, my dear, the games of hide-and-seek, the days of "Now you see me, now you don't" are over. I haven't spent ten years playing the role of the desirable woman one minute and the comforting mother the next for nothing; pitting my wits against the law, always with the fear of being caught. All that is over too.

* * *

A fine drizzle blurs the light from the streetlamp. All is quiet in the neighbourhood.

The church door is ajar. A man appears in the doorway, turns towards the facade. Its contours, softened by the rain and the darkness hold his attention. His gaze returns to the door. He studies it for a long time, shakes his head as if trying to get rid of the web of memories; then descends heavily, one step at a time.

He walks along the wet sidewalk, paying no attention to the drops of rain soaking his face and his hands, which he holds palm up at chest level.

He barely makes out the shadow of a woman barring his path. He does not see the barrel of the revolver pointing at him.

"Hey, did you think you could drop me just like that, without saying a word?"

"Tara?"

"Yes, it's me, Tara. Your woman or your mistress, your star! Lucky or unlucky, it's all the same to you!"

"Tara," the man repeats in a whisper.

"Yes, It's Tara! Listen to me. The joke's over. You're coming home with me. We've been living together too long, I've got into the habit of it. And I don't let go of my habits easily. So, come on! Drop that poor me attitude. You'll forget it all tonight… I promise you my darling!"

Her laugh ripples through the rain.

The man wipes away the water running down his face. He looks at his hands. Stares at them. All his attention is focused on the gesture they are making. The end of his thumb and the tip of his index finger meet; his middle, ring and little fingers come together in a curve to form what looks like a nest. He smiles as he recognizes the old gesture, the gesture that has marked him forever.

The woman takes a step forward. The revolver held unsteadily against her chest.

"You'd do well to listen to me, darling. I'm not joking. I followed you into your church, into what you called 'your' confessional. But I didn't have a confession to make. Not like you if I saw correctly. So, are you coming?"

The man looks straight ahead, calmly.

"Believe me, Tara. I can't go on. You've been good for me, too good. Thank you for that. But the life we've led was not for me. Your house has never been mine. You felt it and I knew it. But I never had the courage to leave you. Please understand. And let me go."

"Go where? And what will you do? Your white hands

– your long, unblemished hands – what use are they going to be? Those hands are certainly too white for working… You fool! Do you think the Presence will take you back? The one you denied long ago. The one you turned your back on to follow me. There's no place for you any more in what you called Religion. You'd be better to come back with me, enjoy this life. There won't be any other one for you."

The man looks at his hands again. They are as white as if it were full daylight in spite of the dim light from the lamppost slanting through the rain. His hands are still holding something invisible, protecting the mysterious Being that only he can see.

"I said no, Tara. I'm not coming home with you. I don't know what I'm going to do. I'm waiting…"

"What, what are you waiting for? For a sign from your good Lord? From your Christ who rose from the dead? Really, you've gone crazy! For years you didn't want to hear anything about religion. You didn't even want to enter a church, not Notre Dame in Paris nor Chartres Cathedral, and I loved the stories their stained glass windows told in so many colours. You closed your eyes every time some little thing reminded you of the past. And now you're saying that all that has changed. I'm not so stupid as to believe that. And neither are you. Come on, stop being an idiot, let's go home. You're beginning to get on my nerves. And besides, I'm soaked to the skin."

"I don't have anything else to say to you, Tara. Let me past."

A shot rends the silence of the night. The man lies on the rain-soaked pavement. But his eyes are open and a slight smile touches the corners of his mouth.

"The answer!" he murmurs. "The answer!"

Tara's long hair is soaked in the blood spouting from the priest's chest, the blood that is streaming onto his white hands.

"My God! What have I done?... My God, if it's true there is a God, don't let him die... I didn't want to shoot... I just wanted to frighten him."

The priest smiles gently.

"Speak to me. Say something. I didn't mean to shoot. I love you. You can leave if that's what you want. But don't die, I beg you."

"Tara... everything's fine, everything's fine... here, take... my hands... And say with me: Take... my hands... O... Lord."

The Neighbourhood Madwoman

Miss Phélie is waiting patiently in the dock. She is indifferent to the remarks from the curious who have come to watch the show; she can hear them but does not understand what they are saying.

"An old madwoman! And what's more, a pervert!"

They have finally got her. The old woman who refuses to conform, who pretends not to hear when they say, "Good morning, Miss Philly." The lunatic who feeds the neighbourhood birds at five in the morning and wakes everybody up.

The spectators' delight explodes like so many devastating rockets.

"Silence!" thunders the judge. "Or I'll clear the courtroom."

"Your name is 'Miss Philly'?" he asks, with a rather ironic smile.

His gaze bores into the old woman whose hands

clutch the edge of the dock.

"My name is Ophelia Saint-Louis."

Behind her there is quickly stifled laughter.

"Mrs. Saint-Louis," continues the judge…

"It's Miss Saint-Louis, your Honour."

"Well, Miss Saint-Louis," resumes the judge, irritated, "would you tell us what happened near your dwelling on Tuesday, October twentieth, at about three in the afternoon?"

Miss Phélie tries hard to muster her scattered thoughts as they swirl around in her head.

"Well… nothing," she mumbles. I… must have gone for my walk with… my dog… and my cats… I…"

The public prosecutor interrupts her ruthlessly.

"Miss Saint-Louis, you are accused of an offence against public decency on the person of a child. Would you explain yourself."

The peremptory tone makes her shiver.

"There's nothing to explain, Sir. I am innocent."

The look she gives him, her grim expression show her defiance; the nails of her clenched hands on the rail threaten to pierce her almost transparent skin.

"Miss Saint-Louis, can you deny that on Tuesday October twentieth, on Eleventh Avenue, you put your hand, or hands, inside the trousers of Mrs. Doorchay's son? And that you whispered something in his ear? And… you did this to a three year old child who protested against your… obscene gesture!"

"What you are accusing me of is atrocious. I am innocent. It would never have entered my head to commit such an indecent act."

It has been years since Miss Phélie has said so much. The voice of the woman she once was breaks little by little till it sounds like the voice of a frightened old lady.

The counsel for the prosecution smiles derisively, as do the neighbours who are waiting for the moment when they can have done with this strange old bird who has come to live in their midst.

"You did not put your hand... or your hands... into a three year old child's trousers?"

And, since Miss Phélie does not deign to reply, he points his finger accusingly at her.

"You were seen, Miss Saint-Louis. We have witnesses to your sordid act."

Miss Phélie searches her memory. But how can she remember what happened yesterday, the day before yesterday or a month ago? Her memory is no more than a sieve that swallows up the days and hours.

"Your Honour," she says all of a sudden. "I was a nurse for the Ministry of Health for more than fifty years. And I never violated the principles of Florence Nightingale."

A cascade of laughter runs round the courtroom. Mr. Stevens, the Legal Aid Society representative, can barely hide his surprise. Miss Saint-Louis has not condescended to tell him this. Newly graduated from law school, his role seems somewhat laughable to him. All the more so since this old madwoman had shut the door in his face, saying there was no Miss Philly in the house.

"Miss Saint-Louis..., Miss Ophelia, since that is

your real name, would you be so kind as to tell us how you came to be called Miss Philly?"

The prosecutor is on his feet in a trice.

"Your Honour, there is no relationship between the name the accused is known by in the neighbourhood and the charge."

In one stroke, he has destroyed the defence lawyer's carefully constructed case. The case he has developed like a stage play. After all he loves theatre. The opening act, portraying the character's psyche; the second, moving towards the climax, the indecent act; and finally, in the third and final act, the resolution of the conflict by stressing the age of the accused, her solitary existence and her strange habits. Here he would have to build on the pathos, arouse their sympathy, yes, at all costs he has to appeal to their emotions. For how can they possibly believe that Miss Ophelia or Philly is innocent? The birds she attracts around her house, her conversations with the neighbourhood cats and goodness knows what else!

Miss Philly is no longer listening. Not to the prosecutor's learned submission, nor the testimony of witnesses who seem to go on forever. And not even Mr. Stevens' *in extremis* plea.

Nevertheless, in a brief moment of clarity, she manages to dredge up the unfortunate walk from the debris of her memory.

"Your Honour" (she refuses to address the prosecutor who is lying in wait for her like a cat for a mouse, or her own lawyer who is stroking his thin, pale moustache)

"Your Honour, that day I was taking my usual walk… I saw Madame Durocher, sorry, Mrs. Doorchay's little boy in front of his house trying to pull up his pants. They were around his knees. It was cold, you could feel snow in the air."

Her voice fades momentarily but she quickly pulls herself together. And her voice rises, resonating to the farthest corners of the courtroom.

"When I saw him struggling with his little hands to pull up his pants over his underpants, which were far too thin for the season, well, Your Honour, I did what any nurse worthy of her profession would have done, I pulled up the little boy's pants and told him not to be afraid for I was a nurse. All he said to me was, 'Thank you' and I went on my way."

The prosecutor scowls, the judge strokes his chin.

But there were witnesses, neighbours. She refuses to speak to anyone, she talks to her dogs and cats. She picks up all sorts of odds and ends from the street. And then there are the birds that she feeds at ridiculous hours. Finally, she behaves as if she is no longer in full possession of her faculties.

Miss Phélie listens to all this. But, what is the use of explaining that she prefers the company of birds and animals to that of mankind. That, during the Thirties, in the North, you did not throw away a pin or the smallest piece of string. In spite of today's unemployment they would not understand. The poverty of the Great Depression, as it was called, was too far in the past. As a nurse she had known the very worst of it.

Suddenly her face lights up, her heart fills with joy chasing away the years, the courtroom, the awful present. For, in her life there had been… had been… Joe the trapper.

It was in 1935, at the end of October. The top of the mountain was already covered in snow, the ice was beginning to form on the lake.

"The ice is going to set in for the winter one of these days," said Joe to the Mountie.

With his hair braided Indian style, his fringed jacket embroidered with multicoloured beads, he belonged to another world. The disparaging look he gave her told her at once what he thought of her. A young lady brought up in the city did not count for much in his eyes.

She steeled herself and, keeping her composure, explained the purpose of her visit: the Indian woman in the mining camp on the mountain was seriously ill. The district office in Victoria had been alerted by radiotelephone.

"And you are the one who has to go and look after her?"

His tone of voice was hardly flattering.

"Miss Ophelia Saint-Louis is the new nurse at Meadow Valley," interrupted the Mountie. "Since it's impossible to move the patient and the only doctor is a hundred kilometres away, Miss Saint-Louis has volunteered her services."

In a single movement, the trapper turned towards

the Mountie.

"Are you aware of how dangerous this is? There are no roads on the mountain, there's hardly even a track. You have to rely on axe marks on the tree trunks."

Joe added with sarcasm, "I hope you are an experienced equestrian, Miss. You can only get there on horseback and it's a rough ride all the way to the top. You'll be glad to get back in one piece."

Ophelia had thrown back the hood of her lumber jacket and taken off the scarf that covered her chin.

Joe let out a sigh of admiration as her eyes in their turn laughingly mocked him.

"I'm a nurse," she insisted. "I'm used to unusual adventures." And she laughed in his face.

"And where do I come into this story?" grumbled Joe as he rolled a cigarette.

"Miss Saint-Louis is to be met by a guide on the other side of the lake," replied the Mountie. "You've got a little boat for fishing. You'd better get going, it's already after eleven and you're supposed to meet him at noon."

"Let's hope it's not that sluggard, William. He should be called William the Indolent."

Ophelia was astonished to hear such erudite language from a trapper. She had already been surprised by his use of "equestrian" earlier. Who was this man who had chosen to live alone on the edge of a lake at the foot of a mountain which was, to say the least, inaccessible?

"Let's get going," said Joe. Summarily dismissing the representative of the Royal Canadian Mounted Police, he told her to get into a small boat against whose hull miniature ice floes bumped with a sound like the discordant clashing of cymbals.

With this unexpected interruption of the daily rush of school visits, consultations and births, Ophelia was experiencing a sense of peace and tranquillity that she had rarely felt since moving to Meadow Valley.

Joe followed a narrow channel in the middle of the lake. The only sounds were the hiss of the oars in the water and the creak of the ice floes against the hull.

William was waiting on the shore for them with two horses.

Joe nodded to him and, before Ophelia had time to thank him, jumped back into the boat.

"Don't hang about," he shouted by way of goodbye. "It won't be long before it's dangerous to go out on the lake. As for you, William, no nonsense, d'you hear!"

With a sinking heart she watched him move off. All the calm confidence, which had surrounded her, was disappearing with him.

With a broad grin, William helped her mount.

"There's nothing to worry about, Miss," he said. "I'll take good care of you."

Well seated on his horse, William moved easily in tune with his mount. Ophelia bumped along behind him, holding the reins with one hand, the other clutching the saddle pommel.

They followed what might be described as a path which zigzagged through the trees. Here and there, a notch on the trunk of a tree served as a marker. In front of her, William sang at the top of his voice as if it was the most natural thing in the world to follow an almost imaginary trail in the middle of a forest which, for her, was only too real.

They were advancing thus, from one marker to the next, when William suddenly stopped singing.

"Miss, I gotta go back down."

And, as she looked uncomprehendingly at him.

"I forgot to give Joe the mail."

The tip of his big finger touched the bag hanging from his saddle.

"I won't be gone long. Just as long as it takes me to call Joe and I'll be right back. Don't worry. Y'r horse knows the way. Anyway, there's the notches on the trees."

She was so appalled by William's stupidity, abandoning her to the goodwill of a horse, and to markers which would soon be obscured by the dark of night, she did not even feel afraid.

"You're not going to play any tricks on me," she whispered in her horse's ear. "You know, you're all I've got. I've a life to save… and, what's more, I'm rather attached to my own."

A week later, she came back down the mountain. The Indian woman was out of danger.

Joe was waiting for her at the edge of the lake. He did not even speak to William who, hanging his head, set off immediately back up the mine trail after a barely perceptible "Bye Miss."

The mountain adventure was still not over.

"The Mounties have told me they can't come and get

you today. Apparently they've got other fish to fry right now. So, you're my guest for the duration," he added with a mischievous smile.

"If my cabin and its rudimentary furnishings are not up to the occasion, they can at least offer you shelter and a minimum of comfort."

Seeing the young woman's crestfallen expression, he gave a hearty laugh.

"Th...tha...nk you," she stammered, "but is there no way to..."

He stopped her short.

"No. It's either my log cabin or you sit on a snow bank trusting the RCMP will take pity on you."

"Damned country!" she muttered into the depths of her hood.

"Apart from that fool, William, I've had to ford a stream that my horse, completely oblivious to my kicks, decided to cross, as well as adding the job of cook to my nursing duties – and these miners can certainly eat! I'm absolutely exhausted, and now I've got to spend the night either sitting on a snow bank or alone with this trapper."

Joe was chuckling. Not to be outdone, she started laughing too.

"Fine, I accept your invitation. I'll certainly be warmer in your cabin than sitting on a snow bank."

It had been snowing for two days. The return journey down the mountain had been even more difficult than the ascent. The horses had stumbled on a trail which, in reality, was no longer visible. The icy cloud hiding the mountain had chilled her to the marrow.

Joe had difficulty manoeuvring the boat through what remained of the narrow channel.

"Okay," he replied and continued concentrating all his attention on the cloudy water which was already motionless around the chunks of ice.

An hour later, he pushed open the door to his log cabin.

"Come in," he said. "I won't eat you, I promise."

As she hesitated, he added with unexpected gentleness, "You will be perfectly safe in my humble home."

The stove murmured in the cabin's one room. As the welcoming heat engulfed her, Miss Saint-Louis felt her apprehension evaporate. There was a camp bed in a corner and, on the side wall, shelves filled with books. A big volume of Shakespeare's works caught her eye. Who was this wretched man?

"The winter nights are long," was all the explanation Joe gave her. "But you're soaked. The trip down couldn't have been easy. Here, give me your lumber jacket, your pants, your boots and everything else. I'll dry it all."

Without looking at the young woman as she stood frozen to the spot, he went to a cupboard to fetch a checked shirt, a pair of sheepskin pants, a pair of socks and some moccasins.

"Put that on," he said. "I'll go get the wood in for the night." And he closed the door behind him.

Seated in the dock, Miss Phélie, is reliving the evening and night spent in the cabin beside the lake.

Snug in the camp bed, near Joe who was rolled up in a blanket not far from where she lay, she was unable to sleep. Joe too was awake.

Late in the night with the only sound the occasional crackling of logs in the stove, a long howl, taken up by a chorus of equally high pitched howls, made her jump. Joe was immediately beside her.

"It's nothing," he said. "It's the wolves, they prowl round the cabin at night."

And, as she could not stop shaking, he put his arms around her.

"Don't be afraid Miss Ophelia. They will soon get tired. In fact," he continued to distract her, "what were your parents thinking when they saddled you with that name. Shakespeare's Ophelia isn't for a young woman like you. If you like, I'll re-christen you 'Phélie.' That's a pretty little name and it suits you perfectly. Yes," he added in such a gentle voice that she almost forgot her fear, "for me, you are Phélie, just little Phélie. May I?"

She was about to agree when a sudden rustle near the door made her shudder.

"I...I'm afraid," she stammered.

He took her in his arms and cradled her as if she were a child.

"I should have warned you," he whispered, his lips brushing her hair. "They just come around at night, looking for food. They're part of nature too, they have to eat."

"I'm ashamed of myself," she hiccuped nervously. "A nurse... should never panic... They told me often enough at nursing school."

"But," he laughed, holding her tight against his chest, "they didn't teach you what to do when wolves come prowling round at night. You're a courageous nurse, little Phélie, but you're also a very young woman up against the habits of wild animals. You mustn't be ashamed."

Curled up in his arms, Phélie was no longer thinking about the wolves. There were only Joe's arms around her, his strong shoulders protecting her, his heart beating against hers.

She lifted her head. Her cheek brushed Joe's face. Gradually, the trapper put his cheek against hers. It was warm and comforting. Then, slowly, his lips moved gently down her cheek. In one swift movement, he pulled her to him and kissed her waiting mouth lingeringly.

"Little Phélie, little Phélie. You are my little Phélie, come down from the sky, or rather," he let out a shout of triumphant laughter, "you came back down the mountain in spite of the snow and ice, to fill the lonely night of a woodsman."

Standing in the dock, Miss Phélie, impassive, accepts her sentence. She is to spend the last of her days in an old folks' home.

Little Phélie, has put back on the dark blue, red lined moth-eaten cloak. She puts the little nurses' cap on her aged head, calls her dog, picks up her two cats.

"There'll be no dog pound for an old collarless dog like me," she mutters. "But Joe is waiting for me there, at the foot of the mountain in his cabin beside the lake."

And silently, Miss Phélie disappears into the night.